SEPTOPUS

and the Secret of Captain Kidd's Cove

Jyotin Goel is a feature film and television writer and director based in Mumbai. He wrote and directed the animated children's film, *Bird Idol,* for Warner Bros.

Rajiv Eipe studied Fine Arts at Sir J.J. School of Art, Mumbai; and Animation Film Design at the National Institute of Design, Ahmedabad. He currently lives in Bangalore and spends his time doing animation and illustration projects.

SEPTOPUS
and the Secret of Captain Kidd's Cove

JYOTIN GOEL
Illustrated by RAJIV EIPE

RED TURTLE
RUPA

For Dev and Aviva, who, for fifteen years, sprayed ink, camouflaged themselves and scooted away when parentally challenged

Published in Red Turtle by
Rupa Publications India Pvt. Ltd 2015
7/16, Ansari Road, Daryaganj
New Delhi 110002

Sales Centres:
Allahabad Bengaluru Chennai
Hyderabad Jaipur Kathmandu
Kolkata Mumbai

ISBN: 978-81-291-3593-3

First impression 2015

10 9 8 7 6 5 4 3 2 1

I

'RIVE TO A RIPE ORD AGE—REARN FROM A ROBSTER'

That's a strange line to find scrawled on a blackboard but no water creature attending classes in Goa Sea World School was confused by it. Every student was aware that the teacher, Ms Noriko, was a Japanese lobster and had some difficulty with the letter 'L'. So all they had to do was substitute 'L' for 'R' and the words made perfect sense.

'Okay, I've changed all the R's into L's. So what's a "LIPE old age"?' asked Irrit8, just to be irritating.

'Sounds like a load of TLIPE to me!' sniggered his friend, Po8.

'Pipe down!' hissed Rot8.

Now, you may be wondering about 'Irrit8' and 'Po8' and 'Rot8'. What's with those names? Well, Irrit8 and Po8, Rot8 and Gyr8, Delic8 and Pyr8 are octopus names—as octopuses have eight tentacles, all octopus names end in '8'. Rot8, however, wasn't an ordinary octopus. Instead of eight tentacles, Rot had just seven (and a half). When Rot was still in his egg, an accident had glued one of his limbs down and it had never grown more than halfway. He lived in Goa Sea World, a sanctuary for every kind of sea creature—whales, dolphins, turtles, sea lions, lobsters and, of course, octopuses. Naturally, in this crowd, things weren't going to be easy for Rot. Since he had just seven fully working tentacles, the school bullies, Irrit and Po, nastily called Rot 'SEPTopus'.

Goa Sea World featured incredible acts for tourists starring its aquatic inhabitants, but Rot was never considered for four-ball teams, passed over for the trapeze act, omitted from the oct-estra. And all because of that annoying halfway tentacle! Rot, though, was made of tough stuff. He knew he was just as good as the others and set about proving it. As luck would have it, Rot had been swept into the lab of Dr Reena

Renaldo, the Sea World vet. Along with her brilliant colleague, Dr Zubbu Zwami, Reena had come up with unique tools that could be fastened to Rot's halfway limb. All Rot had to do was slip his halfway tentacle into a specially crafted pouch, whip the pouch forward and presto! A tool popped out attached to his limb! Suddenly, Rot was the only octopus in the world with a tentacle that worked as fork or flashlight, racquet or radio, spanner or sword! Rot's best friend, Tumboo, a weightier-than-usual female turtle, offered to carry Rot's amazing gadgets in her shell, and together they became an unbeatable underwater team. They had even vanquished the fearsome killer whale, Rakshus, and had saved the slimy, snivelling Irrit8 and Po8 from ending up as Rakshus' pre-lunch snack.

But despite his triumph, Rot knew that a smart octopus never stops learning, which is why he hissed 'pipe down' at Irrit and Po now at Sea World School. Perched on a coral reef ten feet underwater, Rot and Tumboo were there to learn and were listening carefully to what Ms Noriko had to say. After all, she came from a long line of lobsters with samurai fighting genes!

'We want to rive to ripe ord age,' Ms Noriko said in Japanese-accented Fishy, the language all water creatures speak (though no one speaks it very well). 'We not want to be extinct rike honorabre ancestors. So we rearn Japanese art of serf-defence!'

A thick rope of twined seaweed was stretched out in front of Ms Noriko, held taut at the ends by two large Dutch carp, Jan and Pieter. Ms Noriko raised her right claw, opened its jaws and took a deep breath.

'Hai!' the lobster yelled as her claw scythed down.

Snip!

The seaweed rope was chopped in two and the ends sprang away, sending the carp tumbling against

the coral walls of the school.

'Ow!' Jan groaned, picking himself up painfully. 'I wish they'd warned us that was going to happen!'

'Oh, stop carping all the time!' Pieter admonished his brother.

'That was Craw-rate chop,' Ms Noriko said. 'Excerrent for serf-defence!'

The students applauded admiringly.

'Now, I show how to do.' Ms Noriko raised her claw again. 'Everyone rift craw!'

Lobsters, shrimp and crabs enthusiastically raised their limbs. The others looked confused.

'What if we don't have "craw"?' Irrit hooted.

'Oh, sorry,' Ms Noriko said, abashed. 'I forget everyone not robster. For non-craws, we go Pran B. Tumboo, prease to come up here.'

Wondering how she could contribute to Plan B, Tumboo paddled up to the teacher's dais.

'Defence best form of attack,' Ms Noriko lectured. 'And turtre have best defence.'

Tumboo preened. She had always known turtles were the best.

'And now we demonstrate turtre defence,' Ms

Noriko continued. 'HAI!' she screamed and leapt at Tumboo.

Tumboo got the shock of her fat life. She froze for a moment, staring wide-eyed at the blazing red lobster bearing down on her. Then in a flash she shot into her shell and Ms Noriko's razor-sharp claws crashed against Tumboo's solid carapace and bounced off. The students applauded again. They loved Ms Noriko's blood-curdling demonstrations. Ms Noriko picked herself up and circled Tumboo's shell.

'See?' she said. 'Compretery safe. Tumboo's head and regs protected by sherr. Nothing can penetrate. Even Tumboo's tai…'

Ms Noriko broke off. Sticking out of the shell, completely UN-safe was Tumboo's podgy tail!

'Oops!' thought Rot.

'Ha ha ha!' the class roared.

Ms Noriko knocked politely on Tumboo's shell.

Tumboo's head popped out. 'Yes, ma'am?'

'That very crever, Tumboo, but maybe you forget something?'

Tumboo looked around and suddenly noticed her tail sticking out like a forlorn thumb.

'Oh, sorry ma'am!' Tumboo hastily yanked her tail into her shell.

'We try again. No head, no tair, orr right?'

'Orr...all right,' Tumboo stammered.

'Head in...NOW!' Ms Noriko rapped out, snapping her claws shut.

Tumboo's head scooted into her shell...and out sprang her hind leg.

'Reg, IN!' Ms Noriko yelled.

The 'reg' vanished but a foreleg took its place, instantly.

'Forereg, IN!'

In went the foreleg; out came the tail...again.

'Ha ha ha!'

This was hilarious—much better than lessons! Po8, of course, was not going to pass up an opportunity like this. Slithering forward, he spouted:

She's quite the opposite of slim,
Regularly understudies a whale,
And though she squeezed in every limb,
There's no room, alas, for her tail!

The class fell about laughing, and naturally, that was the end of lessons for the day.

'How embarrassing!' Tumboo grumbled, as she paddled listlessly after Rot on the way back to the octopus and turtle coves. She spoke in Turtle-tongue, the language of turtles (Rot had picked it up from Tumboo and spoke it as well as any turtle did). 'You know it's your fault, don't you?' continued Tumboo.

'Yeah, sure,' Rot grinned. 'I didn't stop you stuffing down that fourth slice of pizza this morning. I should have known there'd be room for either pizza OR tail—not both!'

'It's *not* the pizza! It's all these...these thingamajigs I carry around for you! Any more and I'm going to need a bigger shell!'

'Or a smaller stomach,' Rot laughed. 'All right, let's practise getting all of you in there.'

'Now? But...but it's time for my mid-meal meal!'

'Now!' Rot said, putting on a 'don't mess with me' expression. 'On the count of three.'

'Wait, wait,' Tumboo pleaded, swimming to a nearby reef. Standing on a ledge, she turned towards Rot, nodding 'ready'.

'Three-two-one-*go!*' rapped out Rot.

Tumboo yanked her limbs in. Unfortunately, they didn't go very far. With six outsized appendages (head, four legs, tail) trying to crowd into an already overstuffed shell, there was just no room. The limbs were stuck halfway. Rot grinned; Tumboo struggled. Something had to give. With a 'whoosh' like a balloon deflating, the limbs shot in and out popped six of Rot's tool pouches, inscribed with the letters 'H', 'F', 'H', 'F', 'S' and 'P'.

'Ha ha ha!' Rot roared.

Tumboo's head emerged from her shell, a grin plastered across it. 'See?' she said, 'I knew I could do it! All it takes is will pow...'

Her voice tapered away as Rot raised his tentacles, each wrapped around a telltale pouch.

'Wh...where did those come from?' asked Tumboo, trying to look innocent.

'I'm sure you've no idea, Tumbs,' Rot grinned. 'You look surprised. In fact, you look *shell*-shocked!'

'All right, all right,' Tumboo muttered. 'I give up. I'll go on a diet!'

'Such a sacrifice!' Rot chuckled. He waggled a

pouch marked 'H'. 'What's this?'

Tumboo looked embarrassed. 'Uh...that's an "H"...a *h*ammer...'

'A hammer. I see,' Rot said, straight-faced. He snapped the pouch onto his halfway tentacle and whipped it forward. A sandwich sprang out. 'And how is this an "H"?'

'Uh...it's a *h*am sandwich... It's also *h*uman food, so...'

'Yeah, I've noticed the Lab Lady looking for her lunch,' Rot laughed.

Ever since Tumboo had become a regular visitor to the vet lab, Dr Renaldo's meals had developed a mysterious habit of disappearing. Grinning, Rot snapped open the 'F' pouch. Fries. Next came the second 'H'. Another sandwich.

'Ham again?' Rot queried.

'No, that's tomato and cheese.'

Rot cocked a rubbery eyebrow, questioningly.

'Well...' Tumboo explained awkwardly, 'it's HALF-eaten, so...'

Shaking his head, Rot snapped the next 'F' pouch on to his halfway limb and jerked it open: a fork with a pizza slice dangling from its tips. Then it was the turn of the 'S' pouch.

'Now, this is definitely a ham sandwich,' Rot said, peering at the object that emerged. 'So how come it isn't an "H"?'

'It's the *second* one, so obviously...'

'Obviously!' Rot agreed, snapping on the final pouch, the one marked 'P'. 'And what's this? Another pizza, I suppose?'

But Rot never got an answer to that question for just then there was an unexpected interruption—an interruption that gave Rot the scare of his life!

2

Tumboo and Rot were standing on the reef just below the water surface. Rot's tentacles, wrapped around sandwiches, pizza and fries, were floating above, arrayed temptingly for any creature passing overhead. Suddenly, he heard a splash—something grabbed one of his tentacles and tugged powerfully upwards, lifting Rot off the reef. Reacting instinctively, Rot shot water through his funnel, trying to plunge down into the safe depths of the Sea World pool.

'It's a bird, Rot!' gasped Tumboo. 'It's got you!'

'Don't just stand there, Tumbs!' Rot struggled. 'Do something!'

'Shoo!' Tumboo shouted, waving her flippers about. 'Shoo!'

'Thanks, Tumbs! That's very helpful!'

Through the foaming, roiling water, Rot managed to catch a glimpse of the bird that had a death-grip on his tentacle. It was a spot-billed pelican, a large, powerful bird, much, much stronger than Rot. Despite the desperate force with which Rot shot water through his funnel, despite the jets of octopus ink he directed towards the predatory pelican, Rot knew this was a battle he was bound to lose. If only he had Ms Noriko's claws, he could have chopped himself free. But what did he have? A menu of sandwiches and pizza with a side order of fries!

'Grab hold, Rot!' yelled Tumboo, reaching out with her flipper.

Shedding the snacks, Rot snagged Tumboo's limb with a flailing tentacle and hung on for dear life. Tumboo may not have been very effective at shooing away the grasping bird but as an anchor she was the best. Pulling Rot out of the pool was one thing, but pulling out Rot plus forty-five kilos of tubby turtle was quite another matter!

The pelican, though, wasn't going to give in easily. He had started out on his annual migration from

Bangladesh, heading for the marshes of Tamil Nadu. Unfortunately, he had taken a right turn in a cloud bank instead of a left and had gotten lost, ending up in Goa. No one can travel from Bangladesh to Tamil Nadu via Goa without getting hungry. The pelican had a gaping hole where his stomach used to be and he was determined to hang on to what looked like the meal of his dreams: a fish with seven (and a half) eels attached!

Flapping his wings furiously, the famished fowl strained upward. Attached to Rot's other end, Tumboo did the opposite—allowed her weight to sink to the bottom. Caught in the middle of this watery tug-of-war, Rot felt himself being stretched like a string of seaweed about to snap. He had to end this battle, now! And since the pelican wasn't about to let go, Rot unwound the tentacle wrapped around Tumboo's flipper. The effect was instantaneous—Tumboo plummeted like a blubbery boulder down into the depths of the pool; Rot and the pelican rocketed upward. Triumphantly, the bird flapped his enormous wings and rose from the water. Dangling from his captor's beak, Rot saw the pool drop away dizzyingly below. He had to do something, but what?

'Rot!' shouted Tumboo, surfacing. 'Rot, he's carrying you away!'

'Thanks for telling me, Tumbs! I wouldn't have known!'

'Do something!' Tumboo wailed.

'Any suggestions?' Rot enquired, sarcastically.

'I'm thinking! I'm thinking!'

But Rot had no time for that. He looked around desperately—and noticed the pouch marked 'P' still attached to his halfway limb, unopened. Pizza? What could he do with that?

Still...

He snapped it forward, popping it open. It wasn't pizza after all; it was a cylinder with a nozzle on top. What could it be? 'P'... What was that strange-smelling spray the Lab Lady used sometimes? Per... perfume? Whatever it was, it was his last chance.

Levelling the nozzle at the pelican's head, Rot called, 'Hey!'

The bird lowered his eyes to look at the thing dangling from his beak. And that's when Rot let the pelican have it—right between the eyes! He pressed down on the nozzle; a jet sprayed out and the bird's head was enveloped in fine mist.

Rot was highly intelligent. In a flash he understood how everything could change from one moment to the next. A second earlier, he had been dangling from a bird's beak, looking at the not very pleasant prospect of a one-way trip into the bird's digestive system. And now, a second later...

'Aaaugh!' gasped the pelican.

The pelican didn't have time for thought. All he knew was that, suddenly: throat on fire! Eyes streaming! Wing-beats wild! Feathers frizzed! He opened his beak to scream in protest but his vocal chords were strangled—nothing emerged. No, that's wrong—something did emerge: Rot's tentacle! It slipped out the moment the tortured bird's beak opened and Rot fell, straight into the pool below.

'Rot! Rot! Are you all right?' Tumboo babbled, splashing towards the dazed Rot as he sank underwater.

'Y...yes, I think so, Tumbs,' wheezed Rot. 'But... he's not! Look at him!' Rot said, pointing at the sky visible through the water.

The pelican was tumbling, swerving, zigzagging in the air above the pool.

'What did you do to him?' chuckled Tumboo. 'Look at those aerobatics!'

The bird corkscrewed wildly.

'Oooh!' Tumboo gurgled, appreciatively.

The bird pitched and yawed and rolled.

'Aaaahh!' went Rot and Tumboo, admiringly.

The bird swooped and looped.

'He's either the best flyer in the world or the worst!'

Rot grinned.

A final gravity-defying spin later, the bird stopped dead in mid-air and dropped like a stone.

'Here he comes!'

SPLLASHH!! The bird crashed into the pool and lay still, floating like driftwood.

'He's not moving! Quick, Tumbs! Under him before he drowns!'

Tumboo barrelled through the pool, positioned her shell below the pelican and rose, shouldering the unconscious bird out of the water.

'He's got spots all over his beak!' protested Tumboo. 'You think they're contagious?'

'They're natural, Tumbs. He's got a spotted bill.'

'I hope you're right. Spots wouldn't suit my complexion!'

Rot scrambled alongside and examined the unconscious bird. 'He's not breathing.'

'What? You mean he's...?'

'We've got to get him to the Lab Lady at once! Tumbs, that pouch marked "P"—what *was* in that can?'

3

'*Pepper spray?*' Dr Reena Renaldo was outraged. 'Dr Zwami, you loaded a can of pepper spray in a tool pouch?'

Dr Zubbu Zwami wilted visibly as Reena glared at him.

'You...you zee, Dr Renaldo,' he stuttered, 'h'after the whale h'inzident, h'I thought h'it would give the h'octopuz zome zelf-protec...'

'I don't have time to argue with you right now,' Reena interrupted and wheeled away the stricken bird on a trolley.

The door shut firmly behind her. Dr Zubbu Zwami looked around, forlornly. In a corner of the Creature Clinic, Rot and Tumboo sat in a large tub of water and peered over its rim at the Lab Lady's friend, the man who had come up with the attachments for Rot's halfway limb. Zubbu ran his hand through his dishevelled hair and took off his glasses, rubbing his eyes.

'H'een-credi-bull...' he sighed.

He put his glasses back on and suddenly noticed the two aquatic creatures watching him. Smiling sadly, he walked to the tub.

'Youaaoo diaid gooado, gaizoo,' he said, dropping some food into the water. 'Heeaaii theenakoo youaaoo goatia heeiima heeaare inia taimim.'

Of course, he didn't actually say that, but that's what Rot and Tumboo heard since all water creatures hear human voices as complete gibberish. Zubbu held up his hand for a high-five and Rot and Tumboo slapped it with tentacle and flipper (Rot and Tumboo, of course, thought of it as a high-one since they didn't have fingers at the ends of their limbs). Zubbu smiled at them, straightened his glasses, and then trudged dejectedly out of the room.

'He looks sad,' Tumboo remarked. 'I wish humans wouldn't talk such rubbish! What do you think he was saying, Rot?'

'I'm not sure, Tumbs. But that high-one? I think he feels we got the bird here in time.'

'Oh, good!' said Tumboo, perking up. 'And did you notice something?'

'What?'

Grinning, Tumboo waved a flipper at a pizza and some fries sitting untouched on a tray. 'They left their lunch behind!'

4

December is the time of the year known locally as the Season, when things go mad in Goa. Tourists flock to the state to enjoy its beautiful beaches and balmy weather. Hotels burst at the seams with wedding parties and guests dressed in silks and flashing jewels. And, of course, chasing the jewels come jewel thieves.

Goa Sea World shuts its doors to visitors at seven o'clock every evening. By midnight, except for nocturnal water creatures, nothing stirs in its pools, buildings or grounds. But midnight is the time of choice for every respectable, hard-working jewel thief. Sharad Saraaf was *not* a thief; he was a pool attendant. But he knew jewels like he knew the back of his left hand—the one with the missing thumbnail. Two

years ago, he had been thrown out of his family's jewellery business for replacing a diamond with a cubic zirconia gem—a cheap imitation—but he had never regretted it. He had used his knowledge of jewellery to establish a new career for himself and was doing very well, thank you.

You may be wondering what Sharad's understanding of jewels had to do with his job as a pool attendant. To answer that, one would have had to have stayed awake until midnight and silently followed Sharad as he slunk out of the Sea World employee's quarters and furtively unlocked a little-noticed gate at the far end of the complex. Outside, a scooter idled in the dark. The rider quickly handed a briefcase to Sharad, nodded, and drove away. Keeping to the shadows, Sharad hurried to a door with a sign that said 'Pool Staff Only' and slipped in. Once inside, he switched on a flashlight and opened the case. Stacked within were layer upon layer of jewels, sparkling under the flashlight's beam. Sharad grinned and swung open a wall locker. Swiftly, he took out scuba gear, put it on, scooped the jewellery into a waterproof bag and unbolted a maintenance hatch to the pool. Sliding through, Sharad paddled underwater to the Sea World's prized exhibit—Captain Kidd's Cove!

One of the most popular exhibits at Goa Sea World, Captain Kidd's Cove was designed by the Splendid Speciality Company. The display was entirely underwater and was viewed by visitors from behind a sheet of glass. It featured a mock-up of a sunken ship, skeletons of supposedly drowned pirates, and a treasure chest overflowing with gold and gems. For the hundreds of tourists who admired the exhibit every day it was all make-believe, the

treasure just cheap replicas of diamonds, emeralds and rubies. They would have been astounded if someone told them that more than half the jewellery they so casually sauntered past was genuine, and worth a fortune!

Sharad smiled as he extracted strings of gemstones from his bag and artfully arranged them around the treasure chest. It had been a particularly profitable month for Sharad's partners-in-crime, the gang of light-fingered thieves that had stolen jewellery from dozens of wedding parties. Hotel detectives and Goa's overworked police desperately searched suspicious-looking persons and scanned luggage on outbound planes and trains, but not a trace of the missing loot was found. And here it all was—openly displayed to thousands of visitors! Sharad grinned at the sheer boldness of the plan. Just another week and the entire exhibit would be shifted to a water park across the Mandovi River. The night before the shift, a boat would glide up to the Sea World jetty. Sharad would separate the real jewels from the fake ones and hand over the loot to the boat's pilot. When the exhibit reopened in the water park, the jewellery would be entirely fake. No one would suspect a thing.

Sharad coolly scattered the real gems among the imitation ones, looking again at a gem he had placed in a particularly prominent position, a large, 38-carat, blue-white diamond. That stone alone was worth millions! It had been taken from a pendant owned by a famous film star and when it had disappeared from the star's hotel room a week ago, it had created a sensation! Sharad enjoyed the thought that thousands of people would look at the gem, photograph it on their cell phones, share pictures of it on Facebook and Twitter, and yet no one would know what it truly was! No one but he! Brushing aside the fish swimming around, he left the exhibit. Lady Luck was with him, he gloated. Nothing could go wrong.

❧

'That looks tasty!' Jan said to his brother carp, Pieter, looking hungrily at the gleaming diamond lying near the treasure chest. 'They never feed us properly here like they do in Amsterdam!'

'There you go, carping again!' Pieter said. 'You want

a bite of that or not?'

'Ja,' replied Jan in Dutch-accented Carpish, 'unless you want it?'

'Niet, you saw it first.'

'But you're older than me. Go ahead.'

'You first.'

The Dutch are among the most polite people on the planet and Dutch carp have a reputation to uphold. So Jan and Pieter politely urged each other on. Just then a mackerel that was neither Dutch nor polite, shot forward and abruptly ended the discussion by swallowing the gem, leaving not a single carat to be shared by the courteous carp.

5

A hoarse pelican squawk echoed around the Sea World Creature Clinic. The squawk was not an expression of unhappiness—on the contrary, the bird was quite pleased with the way things were. He had been treated very well ever since he regained consciousness three hours ago. Food had been ladled into his beak, a gently humming box blew a soft breeze on his feathers, the air was balmy—just the way he liked it. In fact, there was an unexpected benefit from his recent troubles: everything that slid down his throat tasted deliciously of pepper! The door opened and in came the lady who had been so kind to him. BUT—she was trundling a tub along and in the tub were the funny creature with many limbs and the fat, armoured thing.

Reena smiled at the pelican, turned to Rot and Tumboo and, pointing at the bird, said, 'See? He's fine! Now, I want you to be friends.'

What Rot and Tumboo heard, though, was, 'Seeaoo? Heeiaa fainoo! Nuaau, aai waaonoto youaaoo tooaoo beeaoo fraandos.'

'She's right!' Tumboo said, grinning. 'He does have a funny-looking beak!'

'I don't think she's commenting on his beak, Tumbs,' Rot said.

'Sure she is! That's the funniest beak, ever!'

Rot shook his head. 'I think she wants us to be friends.'

'Friends!'

Rot and Tumboo checked out the pelican warily. This was awkward. It's always embarrassing being introduced to someone who has recently tried to eat you. One hardly knows what to say. Then again, what if the bird was still hungry and made another attempt at grabbing Rot?

Wanting to get that out of the way, Rot said in hesitant Fishy, 'Hope they feeding you?'

The bird looked at him and, after a moment,

nodded. Rot and Tumboo exchanged a look. The pelican seemed to understand!

'I, Rot,' Rot said.

'And I, Tumboo,' added Tumboo.

The pelican pointed a wing at himself. 'I, Pelli Dada,' he warbled. 'Phrom Bangladesh. Bhery please to meet.'

Rot and Tumboo looked at each other delightedly. The pelican spoke Fishy! Not very well, of course, but then who did?

Reena, though, couldn't believe her eyes! Were they talking? It really appeared as if they were!

'Dr Zwami!' she called. 'Zubbu! You've got to see this. The octopus and turtle are talking to the pelican. Zubbu...!' She hurried out of the room.

'You from Bangladesh?' Rot asked Pelli Dada. 'Far from home, no?'

'I come Tamil Nadu ebery year,' Pelli Dada trilled. 'Good phor phissing!'

'Tamil Nadu?!' Rot reacted. 'This Goa!'

'You off by only a thousand kilometres,' Tumboo pointed out, helpfully.

'Oh, no,' Pelli Dada groaned. 'Musht hab took

wrong turn shome bhere!'

Rot and Tumboo looked at him sympathetically.

'Someone expect you in Tamil Nadu?' Rot asked.

'Yes,' Pelli Dada chirruped. 'The phiss!' He looked at the water creatures hopefully. 'Goa good phor phissing?'

❧

It's strange how friendships happen. At first sight, someone could look attractive, appealing, and all you want to do is to eat him. Oddly enough, as you get to know him better, you start enjoying his company, share laughs and stories with him, and soon, you've found a new friend. Eating a friend would be the last thing you'd do (unless you were really hungry).

In the few days it took Pelli Dada to recover, he, Rot and Tumboo were surprised to find they had become very good friends indeed. Although he had been declared healthy by Reena and was free to leave for his appointment with Tamil Nadu's 'phiss', Pelli Dada was having too good a time to go. Pelli Dada was a great 'phootball phan' (as he put it) and was intrigued by the octopus four-ball teams. But what he enjoyed most was just hanging with Rot and Tumboo. Though he was fascinated by Rot's gadgets and the way Rot and Tumboo used them, what he liked best was Rot and Tumboo's easy friendship. Spot-billed pelicans fly in flocks when young, but become solitary as they grow. Pelli Dada had not had a real friend in a long time. He thought of his initial 'misunderstanding' with Rot and Tumboo and was still astonished by Tumboo's struggle to save Rot despite their belonging to different species. Being with Rot and Tumboo stirred something deep within Pelli Dada, and he decided to stay.

❧

'I have an idea,' Rot said to Tumboo as he watched Pelli Dada swoop in from the ocean. 'You think Pelli Dada could help in the self-defence classes?'

Tumboo opened a sleepy eye. She was lazing on a reef, basking in the feeling of well-being that follows a particularly satisfying lunch.

'Sure...' she said and went back to dreaming of dinner.

'You think he'd be okay with it?' Rot mused.

'Sure...'

'You think you've become so fat that tourists mistake you for a barrel?'

'Sure...'

Abruptly, Tumboo's eyes snapped open and her head popped up. 'Hey! That's rude!'

Rot grinned. 'Just checking if you were listening!'

'Sure, I was!' Tumboo insisted. 'You said...what you were saying was...don't tell me...it'll come to me...'

Rot laughed, shook his head and swam to the next reef on which Pelli Dada had alighted.

'Hey, Rot!' the pelican warbled cheerily. 'Bot'sh up?'

'Had a thought, Pelli Dada,' Rot replied. 'How you feel about lobsters?'

Pelli Dada went quiet for a moment. He twitched his long neck and ground his beak as if swallowing something painful.

'This doesn't look good,' Rot thought.

Pelli Dada took a short hop. 'Lobshtersh, you shay?'

'Yes...'

'Lobshtersh got no mannersh!' Pelli Dada squawked.

'That so?'

'That sho!' Pelli Dada trilled firmly. 'Bun time, I phissing. Caught two phiss and bun lobshter in beak. Phiss hab good mannersh. Quietly go down gullet into shtomach. Lobshter hab bhery bad mannersh. Grab hold of beak phrom inshide. Rephuse to go into shtomach! Had to shpit him out. Bhery bad mannersh!'

Rot hid his smile. He could see the lobster's point of view, though Pelli Dada looked seriously offended at the lobster's lack of etiquette.

'All lobsters not bad,' Rot remarked, soothingly.

'That sho?'

'Yes,' Rot said. 'Octopus that shoot pepper spray not very bad, right?'

Pelli Dada smiled. 'That sho!'

Rot grinned. 'So you okay to meet not bad lobster?'

'Perri Dada?' Ms Noriko said. 'That very nice name!'

Pelli Dada winced. He had agreed to meet the 'not bad lobshter', but this wasn't a good start. Like all birds from Bangladesh, Pelli Dada was very touchy about the correct pronunciation of his name.

"PeLLi Dada!" squawked the pelican, emphasizing the 'L's. 'Phrom Bangladesh!'

'From Bangradesh!' Ms Noriko smiled, blithely ignoring the pelican's efforts. 'I, Ms Noriko from Japan. Rand of Rising Sun!'

'LAND of Rishing Shun!' Pelli Dada warbled, stressing the word. 'My name "PELLI", like "LAND"!'

'Perrirand?' Ms Noriko asked, puzzled.

Tumboo grinned, enjoying the exchange. Rot hurriedly intervened. He knew Pelli Dada's opinion of 'lobshter mannersh' and quickly decided to change the subject.

'Ms Noriko,' he said, 'time for class, yes?'

Ms Noriko agreed and she, Rot and Tumboo dived off the roof of the school reef and swam to a ledge underwater where the self-defence class was assembled. The group consisted of a variety of water creatures—octopuses, crabs, sea urchins, every sort of fish—and they all looked curiously at the three who had just been talking to the dangerous-looking pelican on the roof. Everyone knew that when a pelican dives underwater for food, it's healthy to be as far away as possible! What in the ocean were Rot, Tumboo and Ms Noriko doing, chatting with the enemy?

'Crass,' Ms Noriko said, addressing her students, 'today, as guest serf-defence teacher, we have good friend—Perri...Perr...er...him.' She pointed at the massive bird.

'But...but...he's dangerous!' piped up Irrit8, nervously.

Like all bullies, Irrit was a bit of a coward. And like all poets, Po8 wasn't an octopus of action, either. Quaking with fear, he mumbled:

'A self-defence teacher called Pelli
Chomped up every fish in class,
For starters he chewed squid and jelly,
As dessert he swallowed sea bass!'

'That not right!' Ms Noriko admonished, shaking a stern claw at Po. 'Some pericans good friends rike Perr...' she stopped in mid-sentence, stole a glance at the disapproving pelican, then continued, '...er... rike him up there!'

The students looked unconvinced, squinting

anxiously through the water at the huge bird roosting on the roof of the school reef.

'And even if some *other* perican not good,' Ms Noriko went on, 'I show you how to defend!' She raised her claws and snapped open their imposing jaws. 'I terr you my own serf-defence formura. One time perican swarrow two fish and me. Fish went down perican's gurret, but I grab inside of beak with craws...'

Rot's eyes widened. 'Uh-oh!' he thought.

SPLASH!

Pelli Dada plunged into the water and eyed Ms Noriko balefully. 'Grab beak phrom inshide! Rephuse to go down gullet! That you??'

Nervously, Ms Noriko nodded.

Pelli Dada glared at her, then shot up out of the water and perched grimly on the roof again. 'Bad mannersh!' he muttered. 'Bhery bad mannersh!'

Irrit grinned and nudged Po.

'Didn't see much samurai self-defence there!' he whispered.

Po8 chuckled and, under his breath, said:

'The lobster was mightily clawed
But when faced with the fearsome beak,
Her defence was mightily flawed
And all she could say was, "Eek"!'

Ms Noriko's eyestalk spun around. Irrit and Po may have been keeping their voices down but they had forgotten why Ms Noriko was such a good teacher. Her lobster antennae were extremely sensitive and many a time she had overheard her students' whispered schemes when they had thought her safely out of earshot. Again, no student could be absolutely sure she wasn't watching. Ms Noriko's compound eyes, perched on top of stalks could observe her entire class, all at once. Rot saw Ms Noriko's eyestalk swivel Irrit and Po's way and he nudged Tumboo. They grinned. Something interesting was about to happen.

Ms Noriko rapped her claw against the reef. 'Today we have surprise test!'

'Oh no!' the class groaned.

Ms Noriko nodded firmly and swam up to the roof for a tête-à-tête with Pelli Dada. A test that featured the pelican—this was scary!

Shortly, Ms Noriko swam down again. 'Test about to begin,' she chirruped. 'If student use serf-defence that come naturarry, you pass test.' Then, looking up at the pelican, she raised her claw and, in a quick movement, swung it down.

With a twitch of tail and an angling of flight feathers, Pelli Dada arrowed downward, slicing like a monstrous missile through the water towards Ms Noriko's shivering students. Abruptly, the pelican came to a halt directly in front of...Irrit and Po!

'Eek!' squeaked Irrit.

'...meek...leak...reek!' echoed Po, who had a tendency to rhyme uncontrollably whenever he was frightened out of his wits.

Pelli Dada glared at them, trying to appear as

fearsome as possible. Ms Noriko looked grimly at the two quaking octopuses, waiting for them to use their natural octopus self-defence. But Irrit and Po, the school bullies, the smart alecs who had mocked Ms Noriko's little mix-up with the pelican, were completely different creatures when faced with this feathered nightmare themselves. They were, of course, well provided with natural defences. Being octopuses, they could have:

- sprayed camouflaging ink into the water and vanished behind its dark brown curtain;
- used their remarkable chameleon-like ability and changed their shape and colour to merge so perfectly with their surroundings that it would have been impossible for the pelican to distinguish them from the reef; or
- shot water through their unique jet-like funnels and darted away through the pool at speeds of over thirty kilometres per hour.

But being cowards, Irrit and Po chose none of the above. Irrit had never heard of ostriches or he would have gladly imitated them and buried his head in the sand. As it was, he slapped six tentacles over his eyes, stuffed the other two into the hairy sac that octopuses use for ears and wildly hoped that if he couldn't see or hear the pelican, the monstrous bird couldn't see or hear him either. Po, on the other hand, took the easy way out—he just fainted!

Before anyone could react, Pelli Dada opened his huge beak, scooped Po into the beak's pouch and sped upward towards the water surface. For a moment, everyone was too stunned to utter a word. Then a chorus of shouts in Fishy, Carpish, Octopi, Turtle-tongue (and every manner of watertalk) burst out:

'What's he doing?!'

'He's got Po!'

'Is he going to eat him?!'

'He's a pelican! Of course he's going to eat him!'

'Bubble-hmm-guggle-burble!!'

(This comment was in Starfish-speak, which absolutely no one can understand.)

Rot and Tumboo looked at Pelli Dada streaking upward with Po's tentacles streaming from his spotted bill. Was Pelli Dada going to eat Po? But he was here because Rot had asked for his help—he was their friend! Had they made a horrible mistake?

6

Pelli Dada burst out of the water and, with a flurry of wingbeats, rose into the air. But strangely, he didn't rise more than three feet from the surface of the pool. Angling his wings and tail, Pelli Dada skimmed over the water, gliding back and forth with his beak wide open. Completely baffled by the pelican's strange behaviour, Po's classmates watching from the ledge underwater burst into another chorus of agitated comments:

'What's he doing?'

'He's shaking out the water from his beak pouch!'

'He's drying out Po!'

'I've heard dried fish is a delicacy!'

'That's *fried* fish!'

Suddenly, Rot understood what was happening.

'The claw, Tumbs!' he said urgently. 'I need the claw!'

'The c...cl...claw?' Tumboo stuttered.

'Hurry!'

'Claw. That's a "C"...' Tumboo riffled through the pouches in her shell. 'G...H...I...J...'

Rot looked up again at the pelican ferrying the unconscious octopus back and forth. Rot was almost sure he had it right—this wasn't a pelican diving for prey. Pelli Dada meant no harm!

Three feet above the pool surface, Pelli Dada wasn't going anywhere. Rot was absolutely right—Pelli Dada indeed meant no harm. What had happened was this:

When Pelli Dada had plunged into the pool and glared at Irrit and Po, he had expected them to react in the way octopuses usually do: squirt ink, change their appearance or scoot away. Their reaction, though, was totally unexpected—Irrit had blindfolded his eyes and clogged up his ears and Po had fainted dead away! Pelli Dada was taken aback. He hadn't done a thing, hadn't even touched Po and yet the octopus had toppled over. Pelli Dada, though, wasn't easily perturbed. He had twice won the ABBB (All-Bangladesh Bird Brain) title and was justly proud of his ability to solve problems instantly. A childhood memory floated into his award-winning mind—he recalled his mother warbling:

'Bhether the weather be phoul or phair,
Birdsh of a pheather, you musht take care,
If you pheel phaint, you need shome air!'

Air! That was what would revive the octopus! For a bird, of course, the air was up there. So Pelli Dada had scooped up Po and carried him out of the water into the air above!

'C'mon, Tumbs! Hurry!' Rot said, frantically.

'P...Q...R...S...C! I've got it!' Triumphantly, Tumboo pulled out the pouch marked with a prominent 'C'.

Not even bothering to ask how 'C' could follow 'S', Rot clamped the pouch containing the claw on to his halfway limb. He planned to leap out of the water, using the claw to grab hold of the pelican gliding above. Taking a deep breath, Rot shot water through his funnel and propelled himself upward. Anxiously watching him go, Tumboo stuffed the other pouches back into her shell. She shoved in the 'R' pouch, the 'S', the 'C', the...the 'C'! There was *another* 'C'! Tumboo grabbed the pouch and looked closely at it. There was a little '1' scrawled next to the 'C'—*this* was the claw!

'Oops!' said Tumboo, and looked up at the fast rising Rot. What was in the pouch she had given him?

Streaking through the water, Rot kept his eye on Pelli Dada's approach. The surface of the water was just a few feet above; it was time to snap open the pouch. Rot whipped his halfway limb forward, the pouch opened and on Rot's halfway tentacle was attached...a CAP! Human headgear! Rot groaned. It was too late to go back, though. Pelli Dada had almost reached him. Rot would just have to make do. Blasting water through his funnel, Rot jetted upward, broke through the water surface and leapt into the air—just as Pelli Dada sailed by overhead. Rot swung his halfway tentacle forward; the cap ballooned out and flopped perfectly onto Pelli Dada's head! Pelli Dada had never been more startled in his life. Something—a whatsit, a doodad, a thingummy—had appeared out of thin air and landed on his head. He wobbled and almost fell before he managed to regain control and stay airborne. He shook his head violently, trying to jiggle the offending thing loose. The cap, of course, was attached firmly to Rot's halfway limb and the limb was attached equally firmly to Rot. So when the cap shook violently, Rot shook violently, too.

Like an egg being whisked, Rot whirled and twirled, his tentacles flapping all over.

'I've g...g...got to st...sto...stop th...th...this!' Rot thought, desperately.

He flung out a wild tentacle and by sheer luck managed to clutch Pelli Dada's beak. The rest of Rot swung around and landed on top of the beak, right in front of the pelican's eyes!

'Oh!' squawked Pelli Dada, startled.

For a moment he didn't recognize Rot because the octopus was in a peculiar position—he had landed on Pelli Dada's beak upside down!

Rot, though, had no time to waste trying to invert himself. Awkwardly balancing on his head, he said, 'Hey, Pelli Dada. Need to talk!'

Abruptly recognizing the upended Rot, Pelli Dada squawked. But Po was in his open beak and, under the circumstances, talking wasn't possible.

Rot understood at once. 'Okay, Pelli Dada,' he said. 'I talk, you listen. I know what you do. You think Po need air so you bring him up here, right?'

The pelican nodded, and almost toppled Rot off his beak.

'Sorry,' Rot said, after flailing about frantically to regain his balance. 'I no ask questions, you no nod. Pelli Dada, this urgent! Po not bird, he octopus. He breathe oxygen from water, through gills. He, no breathe here. I, no breathe here. Need to go into water. Now, now, now!'

Pelli Dada caught on immediately. He turned, plunged into the pool and raced underwater towards the school reef, grounding his webbed feet on a ledge. Rot tumbled off, detached himself from the cap and flicked it off Pelli Dada's head. Quickly, Pelli Dada tipped Po out of his beak on to the coral floor. Then, needing to breathe, the pelican sped upward, emerging from the water and alighting on the roof of the reef. He took a deep breath and looked down to see what was happening underwater.

A lot was going on. The moment Pelli Dada had

moved away, the students had crowded around Rot and Po.

'That was scary!'

'We thought he was going to eat Po!'

'Are you okay?'

But Po didn't answer—he wasn't moving.

'Keep back!' Rot said. 'Let him breathe!'

'He isn't breathing!' Irrit shouted. 'The bird's killed him!'

'Tumboo!' Ms Noriko called. 'You needed!'

Tumboo, who was looking on curiously, started. 'Me?'

'Quick!' Ms Noriko pushed Tumboo forward. 'Kiss of rife!'

'Life!' Rot translated. 'Kiss of *life*!'

'You want me to *kiss* him?' Tumboo protested.

'Brow water through girrs!' Ms Noriko pointed at Po's gills. 'No one got as much browing power as you!'

'Yes...but...but...' Tumboo objected. 'I'll have to put my lips on *Po's* gills! *Po*!'

'Go on, Tumboo!' Rot urged. 'This is no time to be fussy!'

'Oh, all right!'

Looking as if she had swallowed a spiny-finned fish, Tumboo placed her lips on Po's gills and blew. In-and-out, in-and-out, she went. In a few moments, Po's eyes fluttered open.

'Aaahh!,' he murmured.

Tumboo promptly stopped. 'Pooh! Pooh! Ptaah!' she spat, grimacing as if she had chewed on an old, sunken shoe.

'You're some kisser, Tumbs!' Rot laughed.

'Blaahh!' Tumboo spluttered, vigorously scrubbing her lips with her flipper.

Ms Noriko helped Po up. 'You orr right, Po8?' she asked.

'Y...yes, Ms Noriko...I...I think so...'

Floating a little apart, Irrit8 looked grimly at Ms Noriko. No, things were *not* all right! Not at all!

7

Sharad Saraaf disconnected his mobile phone. He had just informed his boss, the leader of the jewel thieves, that their plan could be put into operation—he had managed to get the Sunday night shift. Sharad had a definite reason for working that shift: being Sunday night, no other Sea World employee would be around. Late that night, a boat would secretly dock at the Sea World jetty. Sharad would collect the real jewellery from Captain Kidd's Cove, slip across to the jetty and hand over the loot. The next day, the pirate exhibit at Sea World would be shifted to another water park. It was a fiendishly clever plan, but all had depended on Sharad getting the crucial night shift on Sunday. Now, everything had worked out. Lady Luck was definitely with him!

Smiling, Sharad entered the viewing area to look at the jewellery he had so cleverly 'hidden' out in the open around the pirate treasure chest. There it all was: the loot—the emeralds, the rubies, the diamo...! Sharad's heart stood still. The diamond! The large, 38-carat, blue-white diamond! It wasn't there! Feverishly, his eyes darted around the exhibit. There was no mistake. The gem had disappeared! Perhaps some other maintenance worker had moved it? Frantically, Sharad dashed for the exit. Emerging in the outdoor pool area, Sharad looked around. On one side of an empty pool, he saw a worker moving a large signboard. Sharad recognized him at once. Claude Custado—Clumsy Claude—the clumsiest attendant in Sea World. It would be typical of the man to ham-handedly rearrange the jewellery and not tell anyone about it.

'Hey!' Sharad called, hurrying towards Claude.

Suddenly, something spattered Sharad's crisp uniform shirt. Bird dropping! Sharad looked up and saw a pelican fly over him. Unluckily for Sharad, just as he was briefly distracted, Clumsy Claude turned towards him. Claude, of course, had forgotten that he held a large sign with 'EMPTY POOL—WATCH YOUR STEP' written on it in big, red letters. The signboard turned as Claude turned and its metal rim crashed into Sharad's head. Sharad reeled, stumbled off the empty pool's edge and hung momentarily in the air. Then gravity took him by the collar and yanked him downward. Exactly twelve feet later, the concrete floor of the pool abruptly interrupted his fall. A sickening clunk echoed around the pit.

'Oops!' Claude said as he looked at the unconscious figure sprawled below.

Lady Luck, of course, had completely deserted Sharad. For if only he had been knocked into the next pool (which happened to be filled), two things would have happened:

1. he would NOT have been knocked out; and
2. he would have seen a mackerel swimming strangely, jerking up and down.

The mackerel had swallowed a shiny stone that didn't agree with him and now he had a bad case of hiccups! But he was late for self-defence class so, despite the jolting and twitching caused by that undigested mouthful, he made his way to Sea World School.

❧

'I, Ms Soak,' said the sponge in Fishy. 'New self-defence teacher.'

Surprised murmurs (and one hiccup) arose in the Sea World classroom.

Rot's tentacle shot up. 'Excuse me, ma'am...'

'Yes?'

'Ms Noriko unwell?' Rot asked.

'Ms Noriko on leave,' answered Ms Soak, briskly.

'But...'

'No more questions about Ms Noriko!' Ms Soak rapped out.

'Hic!'

'And no more hiccups! I teacher now and sponge teaching best! Now, who know about three "S"s of sponge self-defence?'

Irrit promptly raised eight tentacles.

'Go ahead, Irrit8,' said Ms Soak.

'Yes, ma'am,' Irrit said brightly, trying to score points with the new teacher. 'Sop up...Soak up... and...'

'Suck up!' Tumboo volunteered.

Irrit glared at Tumboo as the class sniggered. Rot

and Tumboo slapped tentacle and flipper together in a high-one. This was worrying, though. What had happened to Ms Noriko?

⁂

'Suspended!'

'Yes, chirdren,' Ms Noriko said gently, trying to force a smile as her former students crowded around her. 'Compraint about perican attacking Po.'

'But that not true!' Rot said, indignantly. 'Pelli Dada was trying to revive Po!'

'I know,' Ms Noriko said, hiding the tremor in her voice. 'So compraint soon prove wrong and I come back. Not to worry!'

But the students did worry. They liked Ms Noriko and hated to see her upset. Though the school principal, Mr Babbar, was a very fair sea lion, Ms Soak could be a problem. Once a sponge took root, it was very difficult to dislodge her.

⁂

Buzzz! The mobile phone lying on the desk vibrated. The Sea World Junior Supervisor looked at it, surprised. The phone wasn't his—it belonged to that pool worker, Sharad Saraaf, who had stupidly fallen into an empty pool and landed up in hospital. Oddly, no friend or relative of the injured employee had shown up after the accident or enquired about him. The Senior Supervisor had ordered the Junior Super to monitor Sharad's phone just in case someone called for Sharad, but two days had gone by without a murmur from the phone. So it wasn't surprising that, for a moment, the Junior Super looked blankly at the buzzing instrument. Then, hurriedly, he answered it.

'Hello?' the Junior Super said. 'Hello?... No, thif ifn't Farad… NO, thif if *not* Farad Faraaf'(the Junior Super had an unfortunate lisp)'… Yef, yef… Farad… That'f what I'm faying, I'm *not* Farad Faraaf!'

The Junior Super looked annoyed. Why was it so difficult for people to carry on a simple conversation? He was constantly running into people who seemed hard of hearing!

'I'm the Junior Fupervifor!… FUPERVIFOR!… No, I'm forry, you can't fpeak to Farad Faraaf! He'f in hofpital… Hofpital!... Yef, hofpital… No, an akfident… Yef, akfident!'

This was painful, the Junior Supervisor thought.

'No, he won't be back by Funday. He took a knock on hif head... Concuffion, amnefia... Yef, amnefia, can't remember a thing... Who'f fpeaking?... Hello? Hello?'

❧

In a nameless food shack on a beach, the leader of the jewel thieves put down a phone. He looked out at the ocean for a moment, then dialed again.

'Bad news,' he said into the phone. 'Sharad's hurt himself. He's out... No... Only he can get at the jewels at Sea World... We'll have to let the pirate exhibit shift to Fardeen Water Park and lay our hands on the stuff there... It moves early Monday morning... So, we plan for Monday night... Yes, Monday...'

8

Tumboo was mad. Normally, Sundays found Tumboo at her sunniest. There was no school and Tumboo could stretch breakfast into lunch and lunch into dinner. Not this Sunday, though. Tumboo was so angry she had even ignored her third helping of breakfast!

'You heard who complained about Ms Noriko, didn't you?' Tumboo said to Rot who paddled along quietly next to her. 'Irrit! And you know what Irrit's mom is like! She barged into Mr Babbar's den and wouldn't give him a moment's peace until he agreed to suspend Ms Noriko!'

Rot swam on silently, lost in thought.

Tumboo, however, rolled right on. 'And imagine replacing her with Ms Soak! What would a sponge know about self-defence? "Sop up, Soak up, Slurp up!" Bah!'

'Moaning about it isn't going to help much,' Rot said.

'I'll moan, I'll grumble, I'll complain! Unless they get Ms Noriko back I'll object, protest and bellyache!'

'You've got the belly for it, all right!' grinned Rot.

'It's not funny! And anyway, I don't see you doing much about it!'

'That's because while you've been moaning and muttering, I've been thinking.' Rot looked at Tumboo. 'And, I've got a plan!'

'A plan? A plan to get Ms Noriko back?'

Rot nodded.

'A plan to squelch, squash and squiflicate Irrit?'

'All those.'

Tumboo threw her flippers around Rot and whirled him about. 'I knew you'd do it! If I had to choose between your brain and pizza, I'd take your brain, every time!'

'Really?' Rot asked, after he got his breath back.

'Well, no,' Tumboo confessed. 'But it's close!'

Rot laughed. 'All right. This is what we do...'

But just as Rot was about to reveal his plan, something red scooted past, distracting him. It was a lobster, obviously in a hurry, scurrying along the floor of the pool.

'Was that Ms Noriko?' Rot asked Tumboo.

'Ms Nor— ? Where?'

Rot pointed at the scuttling lobster. 'She seems worried. C'mon, Tumbs.'

Rot and Tumboo hurried after the scampering shellfish.

'It's Mr Yamura, Ms Noriko's husband,' Rot said, noting the male swimmerets on the lobster's tail, as they got closer.

They sped up and were soon alongside Mr Yamura.

'Hi, Mr Yamura,' Rot said politely.

'No time talk, no time talk!' Mr Yamura's eyestalks darted everywhere as if looking for something.

'Everything all right, sir?' Rot asked.

'How Ms Noriko?' Tumboo queried.

'Ms Noriko gone!' Mr Yamura replied, looking really worried.

'Gone? Where?' Rot and Tumboo exclaimed together.

'Not know!' Mr Yamura's eyestalks swung and antennae swivelled. 'I rook for her, rook everywhere! She gone!'

'But where...why?'

'Some octopuses come our home,' Mr Yamura answered. 'Students' parents. Brame Ms Noriko for perican probrem. Say Ms Noriko bad teacher. Ms Noriko very sad. After they go, I go out. When I come back, Ms Noriko gone!' He looked very upset and sniffed loudly.

Tumboo's soft heart melted. 'No cry, Mr Yamura,' she said, gently.

'I no cry,' Mr Yamura sniffed again. 'I try to sniff Ms Noriko's scent. Robster find other robster through scent of pee!'

Rot and Tumboo looked at each other.

'Pee?'

'Yes. I shoot pee, too,' Mr Yamura said, hopefully. 'Maybe, Ms Noriko find me!'

Rot and Tumboo moved back, hurriedly. They wanted to help, but perhaps not quite in Mr Yamura's way. The lobster scurried away, still sniffing.

'Irrit and Po!' Tumboo growled, getting angry all

over again. 'I'm sure those were Irrit and Po's parents! Rot, we've got to teach them a lesson! Your plan...'

'Forget the plan!'

'What? Why...?'

'Ms Noriko! This is urgent, Tumbs! Something could have happened to her. We've got to find her as quickly as we can.'

Tumboo nodded at once. Rot was absolutely right—this was much more important. The two friends swam quickly, heading for the turtle and octopus coves.

'I'm going to tell Mom and Dad and everyone else!' Rot said. 'We'll find Ms Noriko!'

Tumboo glanced at her friend. Never had she seen Rot look so determined.

'I'll tell everybody at Turtle Town, Rot! We'll find her, don't worry! And then...the Plan!'

9

Sunday was Show Day at Goa Sea World. Thousands of human visitors streamed in, queuing up for the aquatic creatures' amazing acts. Octopuses, dolphins, penguins, seals and walruses put on displays that left spectators awestruck.

This Sunday, though, was different. Dolphins failed to leap through hoops, seals weren't able to balance beach balls on their noses and the oct-estra couldn't hit a single note correctly.

'What's wrong with them?' the Senior Supervisor asked Dr Reena Renaldo, hoping that the vet had some explanation for the unexpected collapse of his stars' skills.

'They seem distracted,' Reena mused. 'But all of them, at once? I've never seen anything like it!'

Suddenly, a mackerel surfaced near them. It lurched and jerked, and then somersaulted out of the pool and flopped at Reena's feet, wheezing and hiccupping.

'Oh!' Reena hurriedly kneeled to examine the distressed fish. 'Something's terribly wrong!' she said to the Senior Supervisor. 'Get the water tested at once! All the pools!'

The water, though, had nothing to do with it. The acts weren't working because the performers had something else on their minds. Rot and Tumboo had spread the word and everyone was worried about Ms Noriko. Where had she gone? Search parties had been formed (for some reason, however, though everybody sympathized with Mr Yamura, there weren't many volunteers for his search party!). Octopuses and crabs, turtles and seals and fish of all kinds had set out to comb the pools. Every reef, cove and outcrop was examined, every pond and pipe searched, but of Ms Noriko there was not a trace.

A deep snore echoed around the maintenance house. It was Sunday night and according to the duty roster, Sharad Saraaf was to begin dismantling Captain Kidd's Cove. But Saraaf's head had had an unfortunate meeting with a concrete floor and his work was reassigned to Claude Custado. Which was perfect for Claude—Sunday night, no one around to check on him, a comfortable sofa—it was no wonder that the hum of the pool cleaning machinery was drowned out by Claude's carefree snore. Had Claude stayed awake, however, he would have seen something no pool attendant had ever witnessed: an octopus with a flashlight attached to his halfway tentacle, accompanied by a chubby turtle, searching every crevice, crack and cleft in the pool's reefs.

'Check out those bony humans, Tumbs,' Rot said, his flashlight's beam playing over the pirate skeletons around Captain Kidd's Cove. He glided to a porthole of the sunken ship. 'I'll have a look in this wooden tub. Maybe she's in here…'

Tumboo eyed the gaunt skulls of the drowned pirates. 'They sure look starved. You think they're not getting fed properly?'

'They're supposed to be dead, Tumbs!'

'Dead?' Tumboo stared at the skeletons with their

eyepatches, hooks and cutlasses. 'That's creepy!'

'They're not real humans. Don't get spooked, Tumbs. Go and take a look.' Rot turned and slid into the ship, vanishing into its cavernous interior.

Tumboo looked at the dead pirates. They seemed to grin back at her hungrily, as if thinking she'd make quite a feast! Tumboo knew she had to search the area but...but... As she paddled, she kept a wary eye on the 'skeleton crew'. Those empty eye sockets seemed to follow her! Very sinister! Tumboo had seen too many zombie movies at Sea World showings and they were coming back to haunt her. Hurriedly, she rummaged through the threadbare pockets of the pirates' ragged coats, poked under their sodden hats and cast a hasty look at the treasure chest.

'Well?'

'Eek!' squealed Tumboo, spinning around. Her skin turned pale green and she felt her heart hammer crazily even under all the layers of fat!

'Rot!' Tumboo gasped. 'Don't sneak up on me like that!'

'Sorry,' Rot apologized. 'Any luck? Ms Noriko?'

'No, nothing! Can we go look someplace else, now?'

'Just a second, Tumbs.'

Rot swooped down, training his flashlight on the glittering pile of gemstones on the floor of the pool. The stones glowed, their polished surfaces flashing. Rot held the beam steady on the gleaming stones for a moment, and then smiled. Right in the middle of the heap, its bright tints blending with the gems and making it almost invisible, lay a starfish.

'It's Tara!' Tumboo exclaimed. 'She's in our self-defence class!'

'Hey, Tara,' Rot said in Fishy, holding up a tentative tentacle. 'Be here long?'

Rot realized at once that his question wasn't clever. Starfish move about fifteen centimetres in a minute, so Tara must have been there for hours.

'Gurgle-hmm-bubble-ruggle,' Tara gurgled.

'That hilarious!' Tumboo cried and burst out laughing. 'You got some sense of humour, Tara!'

Rot was baffled. As far as he knew, no one

understood Starfish-speak (sometimes not even starfish themselves!). How had Tumboo...?

'What did she say?' Rot whispered to Tumboo.

'No clue!' breathed Tumboo. 'But we have to show we understand her. It's just good manners!'

Rot rolled his eyes and turned to the starfish. 'Anyway, great running into you, Tara. Everybody look for Ms Noriko. Let someone know if see anything of her, all right?'

'Bubble-hmm-guggle!'

Tumboo cackled loudly. 'You crack me up, just!'

Discreetly grabbing Tumboo's flipper, Rot dragged away the over-polite turtle.

'Uggle-hmm-lurgle?' burbled Tara as they disappeared in the dark water.

❧

Light filtered into Goa Sea World's pools as a bright Monday dawned. The water creatures grouped around a reef in Pool D, however, felt anything but bright. Search parties had scoured the pools and reefs all night, but Ms Noriko was nowhere to be found. Even Mr Yamura had been unable to sniff the faintest whiff of his wife.

'I have announcement,' said Mr Babbar to the assembled searchers. 'No school today. We look for Ms Noriko all night so we take rest now. But we make up new teams after three hour and continue search.'

Rot, however, wasn't prepared to rest. Sleepy

though he was, he was going to search all over again, starting from Pool A.

'Coming, Tumbs?' he queried.

Tumboo stretched her flippers. 'You go on, Rot,' she yawned. 'I'll catch up.'

Rot nodded and glided away.

As soon as Rot was out of sight, Tumboo stopped pretending she was sleepy. There was a place she wanted to look at again. She knew she'd been frightened off earlier, but she didn't want to admit that to Rot. Bravely, determined to do the right thing, Tumboo paddled off, heading for that scary place: Captain Kidd's Cove.

10

The Splendid Speciality Company knew what they were doing when they built a roof over the pirate exhibit. No sunlight reached the water; gloomily lit by small lamps that cast more shadow than light, the depths here were dark and eerie, just the way the company wanted it. Tumboo, of course, couldn't have known that the effect was deliberate. All she knew was Captain Kidd's Cove was as terrifying in the day as at night. Luckily, the human on the other side of the glass wall was awake and was pottering with some metal things. Slightly comforted by the fact that she wasn't completely alone, Tumboo glided up to the 'dead' humans, determined to find Ms Noriko if she were anywhere about. Uneasily, Tumboo went through the pirates' clothes, but again found nothing. She looked around. Rot had already searched the old wooden tub—what else was there? Yes; that big box full of shiny things. Relieved to be getting away from the lifeless pirates, Tumboo paddled towards the treasure chest.

'Uggle-hmm-blubble!'

Tumboo started violently. Then suddenly realizing the voice had spoken in Starfish-speak, she looked down at the shiny stones scattered all around.

'Hey, Tara!' Tumboo said in Fishy, spotting the starfish just a few inches from the chest.

'Gurgle-burble-hmm-glug!'

'Ha ha ha!' Tumboo laughed. 'That riot! How you do it, Tara? I not remember jokes, ever!'

'Guggle-hmm-uggle!'

'Ha ha ha!'

This was getting to be a bit of a pain, though. Tumboo wanted to be polite, but Tara didn't seem to know when to stop! Keeping a strained grin on her face, Tumboo waved at the starfish and swam into the chest.

'Hmm-guggle-rurgle?'

The chest was full of shiny discs and stones.

Gingerly, Tumboo alighted on them. Why would humans want to put so many useless things into that big box? Just think how much food they could keep in there!

Suddenly, something rumbled.

'Yup, there goes the old stomach!' Tumboo said to herself, remembering she hadn't had breakfast yet. Anyway, the box was the only place she had left to check for Ms Noriko. Once she'd finished, she could pamper her paunch without feeling guilty!

Rumble!

There it was again... And it wasn't her stomach! Suddenly, Tumboo was frightened again. She shot a nervous glance at the skeletons all around, grinning at her. They hadn't moved at all. But then, something *did* move! The shiny things in the box rumbled and slid about, as if alive!

'Eek!' Tumboo squeaked, her heart thumping with fright.

'Groohh!' came a strangled voice from the gems.

Tumboo froze.

'Oorghh!' another gasp surfaced.

Tumboo stared at the talkative stones. A bulb

seemed to light up inside her head.

'M...Ms Noriko?' Tumboo ventured.

'G...g...g...'

Someone down below was in deep distress and Tumboo knew who it was!

'Not worry, Ms Noriko,' Tumboo said soothingly. 'I, Tumboo. Here to help you!'

'...g...g...GERROFF!' The word exploded from somewhere under Tumboo.

'Oh!' Tumboo hurriedly rose off the stones.

Immediately, the stones shifted violently and Ms Noriko emerged, panting and wheezing.

'What you doing under stones, Ms Noriko?' Tumboo asked, concerned. 'It not safe!'

Ms Noriko, of course, had been very safe until an unusual amount of turtle tonnage had landed on the stones above her. The lobster's hard shell had always protected her, but it had proved no match for Tumboo!

'W...why you here, Tumboo?' Ms Noriko wheezed. 'W...why you no in schoor?'

Tumboo settled on the gems next to the lobster. 'No school today, Ms Noriko. Everyone out, everyone look for you!'

'Rook for me?'

'Yes. Why you go away, Ms Noriko? Why you hide?'

For a moment, Ms Noriko was silent. Then she sniffed loudly. Tumboo took a hurried step back, remembering Mr Yamura and his sniffing. But then a silent teardrop rolled down Ms Noriko's eyestalk.

Tumboo felt her own eyes moisten. 'No cry, Ms Noriko... Please, no cry...'

'I, bad teacher, Tumboo,' Ms Noriko said in a choked voice. 'Students no rike me...parents no rike me...'

'That not true, Ms Noriko! Everyone love you! Everyone look for you since yesterday...students... parents...Mr Babbar...everyone!'

Ms Noriko looked at Tumboo, uncertainly. 'Rearry?'

'It true!' Tumboo asserted. 'Everyone look for you all night!'

Rumble!

Ms Noriko's eyestalk swiveled. 'What that?'

Tumboo looked embarrassed. 'Uh...that my

stomach, Ms Noriko. I...er...no have breakfast yet, so...'

Ms Noriko looked at Tumboo. To help search for her, the turtle hadn't bothered about breakfast! It was unheard of! If indeed proof was needed how much Ms Noriko was loved, how worried everyone was about her, here it was!

Ms Noriko reached out with a gentle claw and touched Tumboo's face. 'That very sweet, Tumboo.'

Rumble!

Tumboo looked even more embarrassed. Really, she ought to do something about her runaway appetite!

RUMBLE!

Tumboo and Ms Noriko were startled. That definitely wasn't Tumboo's stomach! Something was rumbling above. They looked up and were astonished to see a huge claw overhead, attached to cables, descending rapidly.

SPLASH!

The claw plunged into the pool.

'It coming this way!' cried Ms Noriko. 'Get out of box, Tumboo! Now!'

But it was already too late. Before either of them could move, the claw had reached the chest and its lid had crashed shut.

11

Darkness descended like a blanket. Tumboo and Ms Noriko were trapped inside the chest! Not for nothing, though, was Ms Noriko a self-defence teacher. The moment the lid banged shut, she snapped her claws open and hurled herself at the wall of the chest.

'Hai!' she screamed and swung a wicked claw.

Everything, of course, was inky black within the chest and Ms Noriko couldn't see a thing. Missing the wall completely, her claw smashed into the gems. An artificial stone shattered under the force of the 'craw-rate' chop, a chip flying off and striking Tumboo on the jaw.

'Ow!' cried Tumboo.

'Hai!' cried Ms Noriko.

She swung again, another chip shooting away and ricocheting off Tumboo's shell. This was getting positively dangerous! Luckily, Tumboo knew her turtle-defence and hurriedly crammed herself into her shell. One part, however, remained un-crammed—Tumboo's tail!

'Hai!' Ms Noriko yelled.

'Ow!' Tumboo yelled.

She pulled her smarting tail in—and out popped her hind leg!

Outside, the claw gripped the chest in steel talons and hoisted it out of the pool. Moving smoothly on cables, the claw swung over the top of the glass wall into the maintenance area alongside. An open van, with 'Splendid Speciality Company' etched on its sides, had backed into the loading bay. The claw descended, placing the chest safely in the van. Then the claw retreated and quickly returned with the pirate ship and skeletons clutched in its jaws. Efficiently, all the bric-a-brac of Captain Kidd's Cove was transferred to the van. Claude Custado smiled as he manipulated the machines. Everyone thought him ham-fisted, inept—called him 'Clumsy Claude'! Well, he'd shown them! He had managed to transfer everything without damaging any of the exhibits. All that was left was to vacuum up the loose gems scattered on the pool floor, move them to the van, and he was done.

Claude basked in a glow of smug satisfaction. Of course, he had no reason to be either smug or satisfied. True to form, he had completely forgotten that he was supposed to have cleared the area of water creatures before dismantling Captain Kidd's Cove!

Blissfully unaware that he had already trapped Tumboo and Ms Noriko, Claude inserted the vacuum hose into the tank. Like a hungry python, the hose slithered along the pool floor, swallowing gems by the score. And then it reached Tara. The starfish could feel the vaccum's irresistible tug as it swooped over her, its suction sweeping up all the stones around. But, being a starfish, Tara knew everything about suction. She had natural suckers all along the bottom of her body and she stuck them firmly to the floor. The hose pulled; Tara could feel every fibre in her body strain. But her suckers proved equal to the task—she did not come unstuck! The hose moved on, sucking in the last of the gems and spewing them into their container in the van.

Claude finished up and waved to the van driver. The engine fired and the van started to move, bearing Captain Kidd's Cove away. Dead pirates have no opinion about a change of address and the 'skeleton crew' continued to grin happily. The two live passengers, of course, were not at all happy but they couldn't do a thing! A faint 'Hai!' followed by a plaintive 'Ow!' drifted back from the rear of the van as it left Goa Sea World and vanished down the road.

Rot refused to admit he was tired. He had just finished searching Pool I with no luck. Where could Ms Noriko be? 'Maybe she's in Pool J. There's a reef I need to look at...'

Entering the pool through a connecting pipe, Rot swam towards the reef. All at once, he heard laughter from the other side of the outcrop and a voice chanted in Octopi:

'It can only gurgle or hum,
Mumble or just remain mum,

It's turned north to south,
It sits on its mouth,
Is there anything else so dumb?'

'That's Po!' thought Rot.

And there were other voices, too: a mocking octopus laugh and...

'Gurgle-hmm-burble!'

A starfish! What were Irrit and Po up to? Rot, with his halfway limb, knew all about bullies! Angrily, he spewed water through his funnel and shot around the reef.

'Ha ha ha!' Irrit cackled. 'That's a scream, Po! What d'you think, Tara?'

'Hmm-mumble-guggle!'

'Hee hee!' Po giggled.

Irrit grinned. 'Have you ever seen anyone dumber?'

'Yes, you!'

Irrit and Po spun around.

'I'm looking at the two dumbest, most jelly-headed, seaweed-brained octopuses, ever!'

'R...R...Rot!' Irrit stuttered.

Po just looked on, dumbly.

Ever since Irrit and Po had seen Rot in action against Rakshus, the killer whale, they had taken care never to stir the water when they were alone with him. There were no teachers or parents here, and Rot was looking at them in a way that made them ver-r-r-y nervous.

'W...we...we were just going,' Irrit stammered.

'T...to look for Ms N...Noriko,' Po added.

'Good!'

The two bullies scurried away.

Rot turned to the starfish. 'Hey, Tara,' he said kindly, in Fishy. 'Be here long?' The moment he said that, Rot groaned to himself. That silly question, again!

'Gurgle-bubble-hmm-glug!'

'Okay,' Rot replied, not understanding as usual. 'Anyway, those two no bother you again!'

He smiled and moved away, intending to take a look inside the reef. Suddenly, he stopped. The question wasn't silly at all this time! Tara had travelled from Captain Kidd's Cove, where Rot had seen her just a few hours ago, to Pool J. That was an almost unheard of speed for a starfish! Why had she done that? Had she seen something? Rot spun around and returned to Tara.

'Hi again, Tara! Just a thought. You have something say to me?'

'Hmm-gurble-blubble-hmm-blub-gurgle-uggle-hmm-mumble-burble-hmm-glubble...!'

The starfish had never spoken so much! Ever! Clearly, she had something to say and it must be important!

'If only I could get what she's saying...'

Abruptly, his octopus-mind flashed. What was it Po had said in that rude rhyme? Rot racked his brain and it came back to him:

'It's turned north to south,
It sits on its mouth,
Is there anything else so dumb?'

Of course! A starfish's mouth is located on its underside—below its stomach! Tara was literally sitting on her mouth! No wonder her words emerged as a mumble. Rot reached out with his tentacles and grasped three of the starfish's five arms.

'I going flip you over, Tara! And no worry, I flip you right back, whether this work or no!'

'Buggle-hmm-umble!'

Tara seemed okay with this since she immediately unstuck all her under-body suckers from the pool floor. Rot tugged and, smoothly, Tara flipped right over, turning onto her back. And there, right in the middle of her lower body, was her mouth!

'You all right, Tara?'

'I'm perfectly comfortable, thank you, Rot,' replied the starfish.

Tara spoke Fishy! Rot could hardly believe his ear-sac! Not only did the starfish speak the common water language, she was the only water creature Rot had ever heard who spoke it perfectly! Astonishing! But Rot had things other than grammar to worry about now.

'Tara, you have something say to me?'

'Yes, indeed, Rot,' Tara replied in her cultured tones. 'I tried to impart this information to you last night, but for some reason you were unable to understand me.'

Rot, of course, knew exactly why he had been unable to understand Tara, but this wasn't the moment to bring it up.

'I know you were looking for Ms Noriko, Rot,' Tara continued. 'I saw her climb into that large box adjacent to the bony humans.'

Rot didn't quite follow the Fishy word 'adjacent' but he instantly grasped what Tara meant: Ms Noriko was in the big box filled with shiny stones!

'Thanks lot, Tara,' he said, and raced away.

'Wait, wait! I haven't finished!'

'Oh?' Puzzled, Rot returned.

Immediately, Tara poured out the rest of the story, from Tumboo discovering Ms Noriko to their being trapped inside the box and being taken away by the humans. Rot stared at her, horrified. Tumboo and Ms Noriko—prisoners! He had to do something at once!

'Anything more need to tell, Tara?' Rot asked quickly.

'No, but I would be obliged if you turned me the right way up. On my back, I can't help but swallow bucketfuls of brine!'

Hurriedly, Rot flipped the starfish onto her stomach again.

'Thanks for help, Tara!'

'Hmm-gurgle-blurb!'

Rot waved and sped away. Tumboo and Ms Noriko, taken away by humans! Never had Rot been more disturbed! The only human who could help was the Lab Lady. Perhaps she would know where the humans had taken that box of shiny things...

12

PLOP!

'Oh!' Reena was startled. She was in her laboratory, leaning over a water-filled tub, tending to a mackerel that had been very ill but was now swimming around energetically. Without warning, Rot had dropped into the tub, catching Reena unawares. Perhaps, though, she shouldn't have been surprised because the octopus had sprung out of an entrance Reena herself had installed. Ever since Dr Zwami and Reena had devised those amazing gadgets for Rot and Tumboo, the octopus and turtle had become special to the vet. And so she'd set up a special pipe connecting the pool with her lab, a route known only to Rot and Tumboo. They were very proud of the pipe—it was their personal hotline to

Reena. Rot, however, noticed at once that this time he wasn't alone in the tub.

'Hey, Rot!' the mackerel greeted him in Fishy.

'Bakki,' Rot said, with no time for normal courtesies, 'see Tumboo, anywhere?'

'No,' Bakki replied, 'but maybe Lab Lady know. She very nice. Remove stone from my kidney!'

The Lab Lady, of course, was jabbering gibberish, as all humans do: 'Ocolofashoo, osogooida ito seeoo youiaa! Aoore youiaa hiuingryioo?'

Rot had no clue what she was saying, but he needed to get through to her somehow—he had to know where the humans had taken the box of shiny stones.

'Hey, there'z my favourite h'octopuz!' Dr Zwami walked into the lab. 'Juzt the boy h'I wanted to zee!'

'Zubbu,' Reena said warningly, 'I hope you're not...'

'Don't worry, Reena,' Zubbu grinned, holding up a bunch of pouches. 'H'utterly harmlezz, h'I h'azzure you. Juzt h'idli and poha—south h'Indian breakfazt.'

The gadget pouches! Rot looked at the babbling humans and an idea lit up his octopus-brain. He would make them understand! Quickly, he stuck his halfway tentacle out for the pouch-holder.

'H'een-credi-bull!' Zubbu said. 'He'z zo clever!'

Deftly, Zubbu slid the pouch onto Rot's limb. But instead of snapping it open, Rot immediately pulled it off and held up his halfway limb again.

'Wha...?' reacted Zubbu, surprised.

Tentatively, he slid another pouch onto Rot's limb. Promptly, Rot repeated his actions—the pouch came off, the halfway limb was held out.

'That'z not zo clever...'

'Wait, Zubbu,' Reena said, stepping forward. 'He's telling us something. Try another pouch...'

The Zubbu and Rot show repeated itself—but this time, Rot held up the unopened pouches and shook them about.

'What'z he trying to zay...?'

'Where to store them!' Reena exclaimed. 'He's asking where he is to store them!'

'What?'

'Where's the turtle?' Reena asked.

She swiftly sketched Tumboo on the blackboard. Instantly, Rot pointed at the sketch.

'That's it!' Reena looked at Rot, 'Where's your friend?'

That was exactly what Rot wanted to know. Where was Tumboo? Reena stepped to a desk and pressed a buzzer. An assistant walked in.

'Check out the pools for the turtle. You know the one, the octopus' friend.'

The assistant nodded and turned to leave.

'Just a moment!' Reena picked up a shiny stone from a tray and handed it to the assistant. 'The mackerel had swallowed this. It belongs to that pirate exhibit. Give it to a supervisor.'

Rot felt a tidal wave surge through his brain. That shiny stone! It was one of the pebbles scattered around those bony humans. Perhaps one of the stones from the big box itself. It had gone missing because the mackerel had swallowed it. And now the man to whom the Lab Lady had handed the stone was obviously going to take it to the place where the rest were. All Rot had to do was follow the stone and he would be led right to Tumboo and Ms Noriko. Spraying a jet of water through his funnel, Rot leapt into the 'hotline' pipe and shot away. Surfacing in an outdoor pool, Rot saw the man give the stone to a second man. And then the second man handed the stone to a third.

'Fardeen Water Park,' the Junior Supervisor said to Claude Custado, as he gave him the diamond.

'Gotcha, boss!'

'And get a refeipt for it,' the Junior Super continued.

'Ask for a receipt,' echoed Claude, as he pocketed the gem.

'Don't juft afk for it, get it! A ftamped refeipt!'

Rot saw the third man get onto a noisy machine with two spinning discs and roar off, whizzing out of Goa Sea World. Rot was alarmed. How was he to follow now? But Rot's brain was on overdrive and an idea fizzed into his head.

❧

'Pelli Dada!'

The pelican turned around happily. He hadn't seen Rot and Tumboo for some time now and was missing their lively company. The other water creatures seemed to go out of their way to avoid the pelican, and Pelli Dada had been sitting by himself on top of a reef all morning, feeling slightly hurt.

'Hey, Rot! Bhere you been?'

'Tumboo taken away, Pelli Dada!' Rot swam rapidly up to the reef. 'Need your help!'

13

Claude Custado gunned his motorcycle and smiled to himself. He was happy to be riding through Goa's scenic countryside, with the day stretching lazily before him. As instructed by the Junior Supervisor, all he had to do was deliver the stone to the people in charge of Captain Kidd's Cove at Fardeen Water Park. Of course, Claude knew better. He had been led astray many a time by the Junior Super's problematic pronunciation and he wasn't going to make the same mistake again! Belatedly, Claude had understood that when the Junior Super said 'F', he meant 'S'. So when the Junior Super ordered him to 'afk' for a 'ftamped refeipt' from 'Fardeen Water Park', what he meant was *'ask'* for a *'stamped receipt'* from *'Sardine* Water Park'! Congratulating himself on his cleverness, Claude zipped through the lush back roads in search of Sardine Water Park, quite unaware that the Junior Super had actually pronounced the park's name correctly, using the 'F' where it was needed. He was also quite ignorant of the fact that every move he made was being observed from the air by a pair of very sharp eyes!

Pelli Dada flew high above Claude, following him, but he was *not* using his keen pelican eyesight to keep the biker in view. Strangely, Pelli Dada was flying with his head tilted upward, his beak wide open and full of water. He couldn't tip his head forward to look down at the road, since doing so would spill the water out of his beak. And that would have made things very awkward indeed for Rot, who was seated in the pelican's water-filled beak! As Pelli Dada couldn't look down, it was up to Rot to navigate during their flight and keep a sharp eye on Claude below.

'Man turn left, Pelli Dada,' Rot said, and the pelican banked left. 'Now he slow down. He stop and talk to other man, Pelli Dada. Now he start again. Turning right now. Faster, Pelli Dada, faster!'

Hidden behind a tree at Fardeen Water Park, the leader of the thieves watched as workers of the Splendid Speciality Company reconstructed Captain Kidd's Cove in a water-filled tank behind a glass wall. They set up the skeletons and the sunken ship, positioned the treasure chest and casually scattered what they thought were worthless imitation gemstones. The man's eyes glinted. Late tonight, when the park was deserted, he and his cronies would make their move, sweeping up all the genuine loot and leaving behind the artificial stones. It was a matter of a few hours, now. Nothing could go wrong.

Meanwhile, trapped inside the chest, Tumboo and Ms Noriko started. There was a creak, the lid of the chest cracked open and it wasn't pitch dark anymore. Abruptly, the chest was thrown wide open and daylight flooded in. Before the lid could clamp down on them again, the turtle and lobster swam out of the chest into the open water of the pool. The workers setting up the underwater exhibit were slightly taken aback by their unexpected appearance, but then shrugged and continued working, ignoring the new entrants.

'We free!' cried Ms Noriko. 'We not rocked in, no more!'

Tumboo, however, was not as gleeful. Apart from the humans swimming around, her first glimpse on being freed had been of the pirate ship and its 'skeleton crew'. But those were the only familiar objects in sight. Beyond the glass wall, everything was different—the trees, the pools, the buildings, everything! Tumboo and Ms Noriko were not in Goa Sea World!

'Where are we?' Tumboo thought frantically.

How would they get back to Sea World? Would Rot ever be able to find them?

By now, Rot knew that the man below was lost. Pelli Dada and he had tailed the man like kites on a string, following wherever he went. But the man had been going around in circles for hours without getting anywhere. And it was growing dark. Would they be able to keep the man in sight once the light faded?

Claude Custado stopped—he was exhausted. The sun had set long ago but he had still not found Sardine Water Park. Everyone he had asked had tried to direct him to Fardeen Water Park. Thrice he had ridden up to its gates only to realize that he was in the wrong place again! Were they deaf? He had clearly said 'Sardine Water Park'! Annoyed, he had ridden off again, searching, trying to track down that elusive address. Now, as he sat at the roadside, hot and bothered, wondering what to do, a thought penetrated his one-of-a-kind mind. Maybe the people at Fardeen Water Park would know where Sardine Water Park was! After all, workers at one water park should know the location of other water parks. Patting himself on the back for having brilliantly solved the problem, Claude started out on the long, winding journey back to Fardeen Water Park.

◆

Midnight is the hour jewel thieves tend to prefer. And with good reason. Three conditions that favour them all seem to occur at this time: darkness, loneliness, sleepiness. At Fardeen Water Park, lights had been turned off two hours ago, the crowds had gone home and the few security guards that remained were dutifully catching up on their sleep. The leader of the thieves sounded a low whistle. Two henchmen emerged from the shadows. Soundlessly, the gang collected at the edge of a platform that overlooked a pool and shone flashlights on the water. Ghostly shapes appeared below the surface: a sunken ship, drowned pirates, a treasure chest. Captain Kidd's Cove. And most importantly, the thieves noted gleams and sparkles as the beams glided over the pool floor. The jewels! The loot they had so cleverly concealed.

'All right,' the leader said in a low voice. 'Let's get the stuff.'

Slipping on scuba gear, the trio turned towards the pool.

'*Kosha ha!*' A cheery Goan voice rang out in the dark.

The thieves jumped as if they had touched a live wire. Spinning around, they saw a man about fifteen feet away walking towards them. They were caught!

Tumboo couldn't believe her eyes! On the platform above the pool, most unexpectedly, a familiar human had appeared, someone she knew very well. 'Ms Noriko! Look! It man from home! From Goa Sea World!'

Ms Noriko focussed her compound eyes on the newcomer. 'Seem rike others to me,' she said skeptically. 'Two forerimbs, two hind rimbs, no craws...'

But Tumboo knew this man perfectly. How could she forget him when he had almost drained her and Rot into the sea a few months ago?

The newcomer, of course, hadn't noticed the two water creatures in the pool below. Instead, he smiled and greeted the other humans in the local language, Konkani, '*Samke ha?*'

Looking at him in dismay, the henchmen were about to make a run for it, but at a gesture from their leader remained where they were. The leader removed the breathing tube from his mouth, leaving his scuba mask in place, obscuring his face.

'Anything we can do for you?' he asked the stranger, coolly.

The newcomer smiled. 'I's Claude Custado. From dat Goa Sea Worl', menn. Sorry to bodder you. Jus' want to aks address of Sardine Water Park?'

'This is Fardeen...' the leader began.

'I know dat, menn!' Claude replied, his frustration visible. 'I aks for Sardine, ev'rybuddy send me to Fardeen! I go t'roo and t'roo, t'ree times!' He took something out of his pocket. 'Need to get dis to Sardine Water Park, menn!'

The leader stared. The henchmen gaped. The large, 38-carat, blue-white diamond, the stone worth millions, gleamed in Claude's hand!

14

'First, the turtle disappears!' Reena fumed. 'And now, the octopus is nowhere to be found!'

The Senior Supervisor cringed. 'Th...they must be around, Dr Renaldo. My staff is trying to...'

There was a knock on the door and the Junior Supervisor entered. 'Ekfufe me, fir. We've found the octopuf!'

'Finally!' Reena exclaimed, relieved. 'Where is he?'

'In the pelican'f beak, ma'am. Fomeone faw them flying fouth.'

'Fouth?' the Senior Super spluttered.

'It'f winter, fir,' said the Junior Super. 'Birdf fly fouth in winter,' he added, by way of explanation.

Reena closed her eyes in despair. In the pelican's

beak? Could it be? With her octopus, anything was possible...

⁂

SPLASH!

Tumboo spun around. 'It can't be!' she gasped.

A bird had plunged into the pool and was racing towards her. Was that...Pelli Dada? It was! And perched in Pelli Dada's beak was...

'ROT!' Tumboo yelled in delight. 'You found us!'

'It Rot!' Ms Noriko joined the chorus. 'And Perr... and bird friend!'

Rot hopped out of Pelli Dada's beak and threw his tentacles around Tumboo. Relieved of his burden and needing air, the pelican shot out of the water.

'Let's go home!' Rot exclaimed.

'Yes, ret's,' Ms Noriko agreed. 'Perican take us?'

'Tumboo too big, Ms Noriko,' Rot said. 'But man up there from Sea World.'

'He see us, he take us back,' Tumboo chimed in, happily.

Rot turned towards the surface. 'Let's get his attention.'

Claude laughed. 'Sardine Water Park and Fardeen Water Park—same t'ing! 'Oo would 'ave t'ought dat?'

'No one,' smiled the leader. 'Thanks for bringing us the stone.'

'T'ank *you*, menn,' Claude said, relieved to have accomplished his mission. He shook the thief's hand, thinking, 'Wot a nice chap de chap was!'

On the surface of the pool below, the three water creatures had been trying with little success to catch the eye of the human who was a fellow Sea Worlder.

'We'll have to try something drastic,' Rot decided. 'Tumboo, the flares!'

Tumboo reached into her shell and pulled out a pouch marked 'F'.

Rot snapped it on to his halfway tentacle. 'Paddle back,' he cautioned Tumboo and Ms Noriko. 'The flares could shoot off anywhere!'

He took a deep breath, then whipped the pouch forward and...a piece of toast popped out!

Rot looked at Tumboo. 'Don't tell me, let me guess. The "F" is for *French* toast!'

Sheepishly, Tumboo yanked out another pouch with 'F' written on it. Rot snapped it forward and out sprung a little disc with an antenna and a tiny blinking light.

Eyeing Tumboo, Rot asked, 'And how is this an "F"?'

~

'The Finder!' Dr Zubbu Zwami burst into Reena's lab. 'They've triggered the Finder!'

'What?' Reena stepped forward excitedly. 'Well, where are they?'

Zubbu jabbed a finger on his tablet. On the screen was a map and a spot glowed right where Zubbu's finger pointed. 'Fardeen Water Park!'

❧

'A receipt?'

'Ya, menn,' Claude said. 'For de stone.'

The leader of the thieves did not look happy. He had hoped to get rid of this oaf quickly. Now, things could get awkward.

'Look,' he said, 'just give me your email ID. I'll mail the receipt to you.'

'No can do, menn!' Claude shook his head. 'My boss, he want...wot's dat t'ing...ya, he want de "stamped receipt".'

The leader looked around. There was no one about—just a few creatures floating in the gently lapping water of the pool. He smiled at Claude and casually nodded. Claude grinned back, happy that things were proceeding so agreeably. He was still thinking happy thoughts when something hard and blunt crashed into the back of his head.

'That was first-crass craw-rate chop!' Ms Noriko said, giving her expert opinion on the blow that had just felled Claude.

Rot and Tumboo, though, were shocked.

'He hit him, Rot! Why did he do that?'

'I don't know!' Rot looked at the three humans dragging the unconscious Claude away from the pool edge and his octopus-alarm jangled. 'They're bad humans, Tumbs! And they could attack us next!' Turning to Ms Noriko, he said in urgent Fishy, 'It time for self-defence, Ms Noriko!'

15

'Can't you go any faster?' Reena demanded.

The Sea World van carrying Reena and Zubbu to Fardeen Water Park was being driven by the Senior Supervisor and was chugging along Goa's darkened roads at a sedate thirty kilometres an hour.

'Sorry, Doc. The van's made to transport water creatures safely. This is its top speed.'

'H'at thiz rate,' Zubbu groaned, 'h'it will take h'uz h'another half h'an h'hour!'

❧

The leader looked at the large, 38-carat, blue-white diamond and grinned. Things were falling into place, just at the right time! He inserted the breathing tube into his mouth, signalled his men and slid into the moonlit pool. Fifteen feet below the surface, however, the moonlight barely reached Captain Kidd's Cove. Like phantoms, the decaying ship and its skeleton crew appeared and vanished in the murky water. The gangsters knew this was a trick of light, the eerie structures were just part of a tourist attraction, but they couldn't help feeling thankful for their powerful flashlights. In the dark, silent water, their penetrating beams were a relief, keeping childish fears at bay.

Hurriedly, the thieves started sifting through the flashing stones scattered around, picking up the genuine jewels, discarding imitations. Things were going smoothly; they would be done in fifteen minutes. The leader smiled. All at once, something plummeted from above, the water churned and a flashlight was snatched from a henchman's hand! Before the shocked gangster could react, the stolen flashlight raced upward to the surface of the dark, shifting water! Bewildered, the thieves chased after the runaway flashlight. As they surfaced, they spotted the still glowing flashlight impossibly flying through the night air and settling on a tree!

'What was that?' gasped the henchman who had been attacked.

'It's a bird!' said the leader, suddenly understanding. He laughed. 'They get attracted to light, sometimes. Nothing to worry about. Just be careful, okay?'

They dived underwater again and resumed their work, keeping a wary eye peeled for any more overhead attacks. Unfortunately, the next attack came from below. Without warning, a fiery red lobster shot up from a pile of gems.

'HAI!' yelled Ms Noriko, as her razor-sharp claw bit into the second henchman's wrist.

If he weren't underwater, the man would have screamed. As it was, he dropped his flashlight, spewed out his breathing tube and gulped water into his lungs. His wrist and chest in agony, the man rocketed upward. Instantly, a large pelican swooped down, scooped up the fallen flashlight and flew to a nearby tree.

'What happened to you?' demanded the leader, surfacing next to the moaning henchman.

'A...a lobster!'

'And the bird got his flashlight, too!' the second henchman added.

Grimly, the leader looked at them. 'We can't do this without light and we have just mine left! I'll collect the jewels—both of you watch out for trouble.'

He glared at them and dived under. Reluctantly, his men followed.

Watching from his tree, Pelli Dada grinned. 'More phun than phissing!' he warbled, adding the second flashlight to his growing collection.

There was just one flashlight left and its beam was focussed on the jewels. Deprived of light, the henchmen strained their eyes, peering through the water, hoping to ward off further attacks. Nothing stirred but... What was that? Did the rotting ship move? That skeleton! Did it twitch? The henchmen clutched each other. In the dim, eerie pool, Captain Kidd's Cove seemed to shudder with things unknown...

Then...something glinted where all was dark just moments ago. A henchman spun around. There! On the crumbling pirate ship! A hook had snagged the ship's gunwale and something—someone!—was slowly clambering onto its deck. The henchman grabbed his partner and jabbed a frantic finger at the ship. The second man swung around—and froze! Were they seeing things? Or was it really a...a skeleton, come to life, standing on the ship's deck? A pirate hat was tilted rakishly on the horrible head, an eyepatch covered a vacant eye socket, a hook stuck out from an empty sleeve where an arm should have been and terrifying snake-like things slithered out from under the hat onto the shoulders of the threadbare coat. Clammy fear crawled up the henchmen's spines. Icy terror seized their throats. A ghost! Captain Kidd's ghost!

Something snapped in the henchmen. They flung away their pouches, cast aside all thoughts of loot and sped for the surface. Scrambling out of the water, tearing off their scuba gear, they ran. Not very far, though, as something swooped out of the night sky and struck them on their heads. They screamed and stumbled, and blundered right onto the top of Fardeen Water Park's famous Giant Water Slide. Unfortunately for the thieves, there was no one around to applaud or cheer as they accomplished a feat not even the most daring stuntman would attempt: sliding down a water slide without water! Whizzing down the slick metal slide, the thieves competed with each

other in the loudness of their screams and the number of bones they broke as they crashed repeatedly into the slide's government-approved safety barriers. The slide was supposed to end with sliders being flung into the air and splashing down happily in a pool. The thieves managed 'being flung into the air', but 'splashing down happily in a pool' did not happen as there was no water in the pool. Two wild screams and two loud thuds later, calm descended on the Giant Water Slide. The only spectator around was lavish in his praise for the ride:

'Phar more phun than phissing!' Pelli Dada warbled.

Rot and Tumboo were enjoying themselves hugely. The many zombie movies they had sneaked into at Sea World had paid off! They knew that humans were terrified of dead humans and Rot had devised a perfect plan to use this fear. Unfortunately, Tumboo had seen one zombie movie too many and was spooked by dead humans, too. So when Rot said they'd make Captain Kidd rise from the dead, Tumboo had been far from happy.

'Must we?' she protested. 'Dead people take over live bodies. I'd hate to become a skeleton!'

'You'd take years for that!' Rot grinned.

Reluctantly, Tumboo had agreed, but now, seeing the effect 'Captain Kidd' had had on the henchmen, she was glad she'd changed her mind. In fact, she had to hold her breath so as not to burst with laughter. This, though, was cause for concern. Tumboo had squeezed herself into Captain Kidd's ribcage to help lift the 'dead' pirate. It was a very tight fit as it was, but with Tumboo holding her breath, it became positively dangerous. Tumboo swelled and Captain

Kidd's ribcage ballooned. The old bones groaned and creaked and the pirate oath 'shiver me timbers!' took on a whole new meaning.

'Why are you holding your breath?' Rot hissed.

'D...don't want to laugh,' Tumboo whispered, struggling for self-control. 'Give the game away!'

'Well, you'll certainly give the game away if you explode!' Rot whispered back.

They didn't have to whisper, of course. Humans have dreadful hearing underwater—everything sounds garbled. Not only did the leader of the thieves not hear Rot and Tumboo, he hadn't even heard his henchmen fleeing. Flashlight focussed on the jewels, he was concentrating on separating the real from the fake. Something settled on his shoulder. He glanced at it. A hand—no flesh, just bones. Unthinkingly, the leader brushed it off and continued with his task. Then...he stopped. What had he just seen? The thing came back, landing on his shoulder again. A bony finger tickled his ear. He whirled around and gawped. Barely a foot from him stood a dead pirate—skull, hook, horrible, slithery, snake-like tentacles streaming from under its hat!

According to Greek legend, looking at the scary monster Medusa who had a horribly ugly face and a headful of snakes instead of hair turned men into stone; staring at Rot and Tumboo's version of Captain Kidd had no less an effect on the thief leader. He stood goggle-eyed, mouth agape, frozen in place. Then, more from instinct than thought, his flashlight jerked up, pointing at the grisly ghoul facing him. Before the powerful beam could expose them, Rot swung his halfway limb. Attached to it was the pirate hook and it clattered into the flashlight, smashing its bulb and knocking it out of the gangster's hand. The gangster, though, was leader of the thieves for a reason: he was clever! The moment the hook crashed into his flashlight, two thoughts flashed into his mind:

1. the hook was real, made of metal;
2. therefore, whatever the thing in front of him was, it was no ghost!

The leader took a step back, reached into his belt and pulled out a long, ugly knife.

Tumboo guffawed. 'He'll pull out a fork next! He's gone bonkers, Rot! Thinks it's time for breakfast!'

'That's no food knife, Tumbs!' Rot said, eyeing its razor-edge warily. 'Humans use knives to fight!'

'Ha! He doesn't know us! Let's get him, Rot! Er... what do we do?'

The thief thrust his knife forward and Rot barely fended it off with his hook. The skeleton weighing them down, Rot and Tumboo clumsily backed away.

'The hook's not good enough! A knife or sword, Tumbs—do you have one?'

Hastily, Tumboo riffled through the gadget pouches in her shell. 'Knife... Let's see... "N"..."N"..."N"...'

'Try "K",' Rot suggested.

'"K"? That's totally weird... Wait!' Tumboo pulled out a pouch marked 'B'. 'Here it is!'

'"B"? How can a knife be a "B"?'

'It's a *bread* knife! Obviously!'

Rot rolled his eyes, dodged another thrust by the gangster, shook off the hook and snapped on the new pouch. He whipped it forward. Attached to his halfway limb was a drill!

'A drill? Why is this marked "B"?'

This was awkward. Tumboo had completely forgotten why she had scrawled 'B' on the pouch.

'I don't think this is the time for questions,' she said quickly.

The gangster thrust viciously with his knife. Hurriedly, Rot raised his halfway limb. The knife struck the drill and was parried away. To human ears, metal clashing underwater is soundless, but to a lobster's acute antennae it rings loud and clear.

Clang! Crash!

The Battle of Captain Kidd's Cove was on and Ms Noriko's samurai fighting blood sizzled.

'HAI!' Ms Noriko screamed, as her claw clamped onto the leader's wrist.

'OW!' Ms Noriko yelled, as her claw bit down hard on a solid steel watch concealed under the leader's glove.

'...ow...ow...ow...' Ms Noriko moaned, unclamping her claw and dropping off the wrist. 'I think I broke tooth!'

The Battle of Captain Kidd's Cove would have to be fought without further samurai participation.

The duel was on and Rot felt he had the upper hand (or tentacle). He managed to get in a well-aimed thrust, but at the last moment, his opponent twisted around and Rot's drill dinged harmlessly off the metal oxygen tanks on the gangster's back.

'Hey!' Tumboo reacted. 'He has a shell, too!'

Tumboo decided to try the same tactic, turning around to take the gangster's knife-thrusts on her shell. Unfortunately, she forgot to inform Rot about this plan. Tumboo turned and, naturally, so did Rot. Suddenly, just when Rot was thrusting the drill-point forward, 'Captain Kidd' rotated and Rot found himself thrusting at empty water.

'What're you doing, Tumbs?'

'Using his tactic against him! Brilliant, huh?'

'Great, but how about turning when we're defending, not attacking?!'

With half of 'Captain Kidd' turning one way and half the other, the gangster fought back. Despite Rot's nimble tentacle and skilful swordplay, he soon realized they were in trouble. His drill's bit was just a metal rod with a point and no match for the gangster's fearsome knife with its cutthroat edges. As Rot's thrusts bounced ineffectively off the gangster's oxygen tanks, he knew he had to try something different.

'We really need a knife, Tumbs! Check the pouches for a "K"!'

'All I have in "K" is ketchup!'

Something had to happen. And something did!

A van travelling at thirty kilometres an hour may not get anywhere fast, but it gets there safely. Exactly 'half h'an h'hour' after Zubbu's prediction, the Sea World van rolled into Fardeen Water Park. No one was around. To allow the security guards to sleep securely, all security lights had been turned off. Therefore, the first thing the Sea World party did was to switch them on. The dark waters of Captain Kidd's Cove suddenly blazed with light. And through the pool's glass wall, Reena, Zubbu and the Senior Supervisor beheld a scene not viewed for two centuries: a duel being fought over treasure! Clashing blades, flashing jewels, swirling tentacles! Tentacles? Was that...their octopus? Perched on the skull, under the pirate hat?

'Oops!' thought Rot.

The sudden flood of light had taken him by surprise. Of course, the gangster was also momentarily blinded by the unexpected glare, but Rot knew that their ghostly ruse would be exposed in a matter of seconds.

'Back up, Tumbs!' he said, urgently.

Too late! Partly shielded from the glare by his scuba mask, the leader's eyes quickly adjusted to the light. He smiled. Standing before him clearly visible in the bright light was not Captain Kidd's ghost, not a creature from beyond the grave, but an octopus and turtle holding up a skeleton, trying to play pirate! The gangster's eyes glinted cruelly as he raised his knife. Now that he could see, it was just a matter of moments before his blade found its mark. Rot swerved and dodged like a matador, but he knew this couldn't go on. He needed a miracle.

'Rot! Rot!' Tumboo shouted. 'I just remembered!'

'What?' Rot evaded a slash from the gangster.

'Why there was a "B" on the drill-pouch!'

'Tell me later, Tumbs!' Rot said, fending off a thrust.

'But it's important!'

'Okay, okay, I'll bite! Why the "B"?'

'It's *battery* powered!'

'What?'

'The drill! The "B" is for *battery* power! Obviously!'

Rot looked at his unmoving drill bit. To its right was the red power switch. Quickly, Rot reached out and clicked it on. The drill bit turned, whirred to life. Would it make a difference? Rot didn't know, but he had to try. Hopefully, he thrust the spinning bit toward the gangster. The gangster turned lazily, confidently, knowing that the drill had bounced harmlessly off his metal tanks. But that was before Tumboo's brainwave. This time, things were different. Like a shark's tooth, the whirring drill bit sliced hungrily into the tank, punching a hole through the metal. Oxygen spurted out of the newly created hole with enormous force, shooting the tanks through the water like twin torpedoes. Unfortunately for the leader, he was strapped to the tanks and where the tanks went, the leader went!

'Wow! He's faster than you, Rot!' Tumboo said admiringly, as she watched the gangster streak helplessly through the pool.

'Maybe,' Rot sniffed, 'but it's all about control!'

Setting new underwater speed records, the out-of-control gangster barrelled through the water. He crashed against a wall, ricocheted off, raced toward the viewing wall and bounced like a rubber toy off its unbreakable glass, right in front of a startled Reena and Zubbu, looking on from the other side.

'H'een-credi-bull!' Zubbu said. 'By my calculationz, he hit h'it h'at h'eighty kilometrez h'an h'hour!'

The oxygen tanks hadn't had so much fun since they were manufactured and they weren't quite finished yet. Changing direction, they blasted out of the pool and soared into the night sky, with the gangster dangling like a kite's tail. If the gangster had looked around, he would have had a spectacular view of Fardeen Water Park, but he was in no condition to appreciate the scenery. Thirty feet above the ground, the tanks finally ran out of oxygen and plummeted. The leader crashed on to the hard tiles of the water park face down, his body sandwiched between the ground and the tanks.

'Ouch!' Rot winced. 'That must have hurt!'

Tumboo grinned. 'Turtle defence Rule No.1—always fall on your shell!'

As they laughed and slapped tentacle and flipper together, Reena and Zubbu ran up to the broken gangster.

'Look, Rot!' Tumboo pointed. 'It's the Lab Lady!'

'So it is, Tumbs,' Rot smiled. 'Time to go home!'

16

'WAT-ER CATCH!'
'GANG ALL WASHED UP!'
'SEA CREATURES NET JEWEL THIEVES!'

For more than a week now, the front pages had blared out the sensational news. Television anchors had shrieked themselves hoarse about the capture of the jewel thieves by the heroic water creatures. Crowds had poured into Sea World to catch a glimpse of the briny brave-hearts. There were octopus toys and turtle tee shirts everywhere and though Tumboo basked in all the attention, she wasn't too happy with the photograph they had used.

'I look like I weigh fifty kilos in that picture!' she complained. 'Everyone knows I'm just forty!'

'Forty-five,' suggested Rot, grinning.

Tumboo would have objected, but this wasn't the moment. Pelli Dada was leaving. The call of the Tamil 'phiss' had finally caught up with the pelican and, reluctantly, he had decided to keep his appointment with them.

'But why you have to go, Pelli Dada?' Tumboo asked in Fishy. 'Everybody here love you now!'

Which was true. They were all heroes now, even the pelican. No one blamed him for the Po incident anymore. In fact, Mr Babbar had scolded Irrit for making a fuss about it and Ms Noriko was self-defence teacher again (Ms Soak was the new janitor, a job much more suitable for a sponge!). Pelli Dada, though, was only obeying his pelican instinct, and it was time for goodbyes.

'You keep in touch, right, Pelli Dada?' Rot said, bobbing on the water surface next to the reef on which the pelican stood.

'I come neksht year,' Pelli Dada warbled. 'To meet good phriends, Rot and Tumboo.'

Tumboo felt her eyes grow damp and blew her nose noisily.

Rot smiled. 'We have gift for you, Pelli Dada.'

Tumboo handed Rot a pouch marked 'P'.

Rot looked at Tumboo. 'Not pizza, right?' he whispered.

'No,' Tumboo replied confidently. But she secretly crossed her flippers.

Rot clamped the pouch onto his halfway tentacle and whipped it forward. A can popped out—pepper spray! Pelli Dada blinked. His last meeting with that can had not been a happy one.

'For food, Pelli Dada,' Rot said, hurriedly.

'Pepper-fish!' Tumboo added. 'Good manners, good taste!'

Pelli Dada took the can. 'Pepper-phiss,' he repeated, dreamily. Suddenly, he put his wings around Rot and Tumboo. 'Bhery, bhery good phriends,' he warbled in a choked voice.

Then he hopped back, popped the can into his beak-pouch, flapped his wings and leapt into the air. As he rose, he turned and waved a wing. Rot and Tumboo waved back. The pelican flew higher, slipped into a passing air current and vanished beyond the trees.

'Well, that's that!' Tumboo said, honking into her flipper.

'Not quite,' Rot said.

'Oh?'

'You've forgotten something.'

'What?'

'The Plan!'

'The...the Plan?' Tumboo's eyes lit up. 'You mean the one for...?'

'...you-know-who!' Rot interrupted. He slipped underwater and pulled out a seaweed-wrapped bundle from a narrow niche in the reef.

'What's that?' asked Tumboo, eyeing the package curiously.

Rot held the pouch aloft, displaying the prominent 'P' marked on its side. 'The master plot to hook, line and sink you-know-who!'

'But...but why keep it here?' protested Tumboo. 'Why not in my shell with the pouches?'

'Because it's a secret,' Rot said. He slid the package back into the niche and glided away from the reef. 'We can't let you-know-who get their grubby tentacles on what's inside.' He vanished behind a clump of seaweed.

'But look here, Rot...' Tumboo said, barrelling after Rot.

A tentacle shot out, grabbed the turtle and yanked her down.

'What...?'

Rot raised a tentacle to his beak and pointed through the seaweed with another. Tumboo turned to look. Two shadowy forms slipped out from behind the reef that Rot and Tumboo had just left and floated up to the niche within which Rot had hidden the bundle.

'That's Irrit and Po...' began Tumboo.

Rot clapped a tentacle onto her mouth. 'Just watch,' he whispered.

Crowing with triumph, Irrit and Po pulled the bundle out of the niche.

Chortling with glee, Irrit and Po ripped the bundle open.

'Urrrghhh!' gasped Irrit as a piercing fluid shot into his eyes.

'Grooooghh!' gagged Po as the pungent fluid clogged his gills.

The sharp smell of ammonia spread as the fluid covered every inch of the terrible twosome. Coughing, wheezing, weeping, Irrit and Po fled, trailing an overpowering stench.

'Ugh...they stink!' Tumboo turned to Rot. 'What *was* in that bundle?'

Rot grinned. 'The "P" on the package...it didn't stand for "Plan".'

'No? Then, what...?'

'A contribution from Mr Yamura!'

'What? You mean...?'

Rot nodded.

'Ha ha ha ha!' yelled Tumboo. 'Now *that's* a Plan! Ha ha ha! Poor Irrit! Poor Po! Ha ha ha ha ha!'

www.ingramcontent.com/pod-product-compliance
Lightning Source LLC
LaVergne TN
LVHW091000080826
845145LV00003B/1069

* 9 7 8 8 1 2 9 1 3 5 9 3 3 *